WILLOW'S WARRIORS AND THE DISTURBERS

WILLOW'S WARRIORS AND THE DISTURBERS

Lynn Farmer

Willow's Warriors and The Disturbers

Published by BooxAI
ISBN: 978-965-578-590-6

BooX AI

Acknowledgments

I would like to thank everyone who was involved in the creation of this book, especially my family for all their love, support, faith and belief in me along the way!

I hope to inspire, influence and guide today's young people to take direct action in transforming the world, becoming heroes in the fight to save the planet!

Chapter 1

We Exist!

"We must be willing to let go of the life we planned so as to have the life that is waiting for us." – Joseph Campbell

Willow Branch O'Brien was a young girl who lived out of doors in her own tomboyish way. Her thick brown locks were strewn in a tangled mess in every direction and blew wild and free in the warm, southern breeze. She was independent and high-spirited. Wearing an old, faded pair of jeans and a holey tee shirt while loving the natural world. Willow adored nature. She was drawn to the glow of lightning bugs that flickered while illuminating the night sky. As she leisurely strolled through a field brim full of Goldenrods, feeling the rich, dark soil under her fingernails, the endless hours ticked by searching, exploring and discovering the magnificent wonders of her home state. This was her passion.

Born into a multi-generational mining family, the O'Briens had labored in the hills and caverns of Kentucky for decades, digging coal from the ground for a living. Their ancestry was forged through migration from Ireland, then to Scotland and finally to the United States. They were closely tethered in an organic and contractual way to the earth. This was the only life they knew. Father Daniel and older brother Paul, were employed in the underground extraction industry, as few other occupations were available. Born out of necessity, it was the only practical work option an able-bodied individual had. The locals could hardly do anything else that didn't involve working the land. Mining was a way of life. It was a backbreaking profession and posed hazardous, long-term health consequences that affected Willow's childhood in a distinctly dark way.

While she was growing up, Willow would go down into the mines with Daniel and Paul to carry coal for heating their home. From a tender age, she knew that coal was a substance that could be burned to generate electricity and was used in the making of iron ore for steel production. She heard her family talk about these things. Coal was an essential material, because people were dependent on it and regarded it as a much-needed source of energy, being a highly valuable commodity in the United States.

The small city of Ashland, Kentucky, was home to her. Not only was the area's economy deeply dependent on underground coal mining, Kentucky's gross domestic product was primarily focused on all types of mining as well. This meant that her family and the majority of other families could only survive by doing this kind of labor-intensive work. Miners suffered many health risks and dangers. They breathed in coal dust and developed medical problems such as the Black Lung disease. Life was hazardous and a heavy toll was taken on the population. Many miners died prematurely.

As a small girl, Willow would see her father trudge off each morning to the mines. He would come home every night, sooty, with a powdery blanket of dust covering his entire body from head to toe. This sight distressed her so much, never understanding why he was so dirty.

He explained to her, "I must dig coal out of the ground so people have fuel to heat their homes. We use it in our own home too, dearest."

Tears streamed down her face as she spoke, "I don't like it, Daddy! I can't hug you when you're like that!"

Daniel knelt on one knee to be close to his daughter while he gently cradled her face in his hands. "Some day, Sweetheart, I won't have to do this kind of work anymore and then I can stay at home with you. But, for now, don't be sad, little one. Everything will be alright. I love you very much, darlin'."

Leaping into her father's arms, she hugged him with all her might. At that moment, it didn't matter how he looked. As the thick ashen dust hung, casting him in a dark shadow-like shroud, she coiled her body tightly around his waist, gently resting her head on his shoulder to be as close to him as possible. Being back home and safe was all that mattered. The fond memories of nature and family carried her for years to come up to the time when she needed to choose a career.

The mining industry became less and less appealing while growing up. She knew from personal experience that its impact on her community was unpleasant. The myriad negative social effects and environmental degradation were devastating. During high school, a local organization, Kentucky First, made a presentation about their activities to the students. They were dedicated to the mission of protecting the state's natural resources through environmental activism. This organization appealed to her core values, which were centered on her abiding appreciation of the natural world.

Willow was strongly motivated to join the cause at a young age. She was brought up in a small, closely knit, neighborly community. She had a deep love of nature and the outdoors; what better way to serve and give back to the community and state she loved so dearly? She knew in her bones that protecting the wonders of nature and receiving an education in environmental activism at the same time made perfect sense.

During her junior year in high school, Willow worked as an intern. Her primary duties involved increasing her awareness and advocacy skills and strengthening her commitment to supporting and promoting clean energy across the state. She learned about hydraulic fracking. This was a practice that the organization deemed unstable.

Willow became a full-fledged member of Kentucky First in her mid teenage years. She enjoyed learning about the environment and how to protect delicate ecosystems through direct action. She became keenly aware of the harmful elements and recognized the caustic influences they had. She saw how wealthy corporations and politicians exerted power and control over people and places while they damaged the environment for profit and greed.

Rural communities, such as Willow's, were often targeted and exploited for the disposal of industrial waste and other hazardous materials. Corporations viewed these communities as worthless and unimportant and put them into an expendable category. The corporations used these rural communities as toxic dumping grounds. These eye-opening experiences colored Willow's world. She knew a little before, but much more now, with a feeling poised to gain a deeper knowledge that would take on new meaning as the next chapter of her life started to unfold.

It was a typical weekend during the school break at the Christmas holiday. Snow blanketed the roads, the smell of cookies lingered in the streets, and people were full of unmatched cheer. Willow was helping her brother Paul collect coal from one of the local mines. She relished spending as much time as possible with him, even though it was unpleasant for her to be in constricted spaces.

As she was trailing closely behind him and down a long corridor that led to an intersection between tunnels,

Willow heard a sound that could only be described as an eerie, high-pitched buzzing noise.

"Paul, did you hear that?" Willow asked.

He turned around, while simultaneously shaking his head no, "You're just hearing the oil lamp hissing under pressure...that's all. Forget it, Sis. There's nothing to be afraid of."

Willow breathed a sigh of relief and relaxed for a moment as she calmly deferred to her brother's expertise in these matters. She pushed the thought out of her head and chalked it up to an active imagination. The sound repeated as if perfectly timed. Willow heard it clearly, except now, it was much louder.

Plodding along and oblivious to the noise, Paul stared straight ahead. He was unbothered as he kept a steady pace toward the pit and focused on the task at hand. Willow's curiosity got the better of her and the sound kept demanding her attention. So, she decided to hang back a bit and wait for the chance to hear it again. Paul disappeared from sight. In an instant, the light turned from dim to completely black.

Alone in the pitch-black darkness, Willow whispered in a frightened, timid voice that was barely audible, "Paul...is that you?"

The reply was a woman's voice that echoed back! Willow gasped asking breathlessly, "Who...who are you?'

"I'm your Mother," was the deliberate response.

Willow could hardly believe what she was hearing. "My...my Mother?" she said, stunned and amazed.

"Yes, dear...your Mother Earth." In the blink of an eye, there was a bright, blinding light that outlined an unusual image on the cavern wall. A youngish woman appeared dressed in white. Green and brown foliage was woven into her hair. It encircled her shoulders and flowed leisurely down her back.

Willow stood still, mouth wide open, mesmerized as she gazed upon the apparition. "Are you real... are... are you... a spirit?"

"Yes, dear, I'm the spirit of Nature, the guardian of the Earth. I must appear when the survival of the planet is at risk. At the present time, there are aggressive and hostile forces that are rapidly destroying the health of this world! The air, water, land and all living beings are being damaged at a rate that will ultimately cause annihilation! A major species loss has already begun on a substantial scale! I witnessed the almost total demise of the planet only once before, and that was over 2.4 million years ago," she said with a pained look on her face.

Willow's mind could barely imagine a million years ago. She stuttered: "Wait…what? Why is this never talked about?"

The Oracle stood erect as she continued. "It was during a time that humans called The Ice Age. The Pleistocene Period occurred due to massive instabilities, which brought about climate changes. A global winter phenomenon, accompanied by volatile geologic activity, took place. The result was a catastrophic occurrence that brought about an almost total end of the majority of life on Earth."

Willow took a moment to catch her breath.

"At the present time, human beings and their industrial folly are at fault for creating similar conditions. They're depleting oxygen levels necessary to sustain life, killing trees and contributing to wildfires; these actions are leading to the destruction of the forests. Unnatural substances, such as plastics and chemicals, are littering and destroying the oceans. As human overpopulation is polluting the Earth and devastating natural resources, increased burdens are placed on vulnerable plant life and animal ecosystems."

Willow listened intently and was in complete and total amazement. "Why have you appeared to me, Mother?"

The Oracle replied, "I have been observing you since you were a little child, Willow. You have a strength of character that is seldom seen in a person your age. A powerful, reverent love for the Earth abides in you. Your compassionate concern for others is most evident. This is a rare quality in one so young. You have demonstrated an active involvement in your community and a deep devotion to your family. I believe you're someone who can inspire people to take action and change for the better."

Incredulous and baffled by what she heard, Willow wondered if this could really be happening or if she was imagining it all? The air was quite thin in the tunnels. The possibility of hallucinating crossed her mind.

Nothing felt out of the ordinary. She was not lightheaded or shaky.

Willow inquired of The Oracle, "What do you want of me? What can I do? How can I help?"

"A great deal is required of you. You can take on the task of forming a group dedicated to saving the planet. These members will travel around the world and stand up to all those who are actively destroying the Earth. They will respond to crises on many fronts before it is too late!"

Willow asked, "Will you be with us, Mother?"

"No, not always," she replied. "I can only be present in this form for short periods of time when we come together to talk. You can reach me from your heart space and through a conviction of love for the planet and belief in its survival. If you need my help, just say, We Exist! That will cause me to materialize."

Without any fanfare, she faded away just as suddenly as she had appeared. Plunging the cavern into total darkness again, slowly the light from the oil lamp began to come back up. It hissed and sputtered. Willow sank slowly to her knees, feeling weak and half-dazed from the strange encounter, but sensed intuitively it must have been real.

Willow noticed the dim glow of a swinging lantern coming toward her from the far end of the tunnel. *Oh no, it must be Paul!* She wondered. What can I tell him I've been doing all this time? It was quite a dilemma. Willow knew he'd never comprehend what had happened, since she barely did herself. It was impossible to understand this strange encounter. She decided not to tell Paul what had really happened. Willow knew her life would be changed forever. At this moment, though, it was unclear to her just how much.

When he appeared in the opening of the passageway leading to the main tunnel, he was dragging a large satchel of coal tied to a rope behind him. She could see a look of brotherly concern etched on his face.

"Where were you? Where have you been, Sis? Yeah, I know. I really wasn't super worried since you're so curious about everything, but I did wonder what made you stay behind," Paul asked casually.

Willow shrugged her shoulders and searched nervously for an answer. "I was just tired, Paul, so I paused for a short rest. Then when I turned around, you were gone. I decided to wait here for you rather than trying to go on alone."

Paul wore a satisfied smile and was content with her answer. He brushed away the coal dust from his little sister's clothes as he helped her up. "Mom and Dad will be wondering where we are by now...ready to go home and get warm, kiddo?" Willow responded with a resounding "Yes!" She was relieved, wide-eyed and alert. The unbelievable events had set her feet on a path that would forever change her worldview. Her faith in the message would make all the difference for Willow in the events to come.

The winters in Kentucky could be quite long as the ample snowfall lasted well into spring. That particular day, the journey from the coal mine seemed like the longest walk she'd ever taken. Staying close to Paul, Willow swept the long strands of wet hair aside in order to clear her line of sight, staying focused on the path, while following closely in his footsteps. Many questions raced through her mind, which were left unanswered from the auspicious encounter that morning. The biggest one was: *why was I chosen for such a mission?* Without fully comprehending the answer or understanding such an unusual experience, it baffled the senses that it ever actually happened. Although it was impossible to deny, she interpreted it as some sort of calling to an unknown higher purpose. It was clear, though, that her next steps would have to be taken with sheer determination alone.

Chapter 2

United We Stand!

"Alone, we can do so little; together, we can do so much." – Helen Keller

When she saw the house she was brought up in, it provided a powerful sense of relief. Willow was back in the bosom of the family that raised her. She was sheltered in a safe, comfortable and secure space. Home was the most beautiful place in the world, especially during the holidays. She was close to those she loved and enjoying the spirit of the season. Their world was abundant and overflowing with cheer. The smells of Betsy's southern cooking wafted from the kitchen, while Paul and Daniel took turns tending the coal burner. The Christmas tree was shining brightly and Ginger was sleeping soundly in her bed. Willow hoped that tonight she'd be accepted for whatever choices she needed to make.

In light of the day's events, she gathered the strength to discuss her ideas at dinner. It had always made sense in the past to get everyone's opinion and feedback before making important life-changing plans. Willow earnestly considered how she would open up to her family. *What would she say?* The time to tell them was now. It was not an option to carefully select what she wanted to say while deciding to speak. How could she justify being away from school and explain, out of the blue, that she wanted to assemble a group of young people to take on the enormous task of protecting and cleaning up the planet?

At dusk, the family came together for the sumptuous meal Betsy had prepared. Willow was never much help in the kitchen, so her mother, although very traditional, didn't insist she learn to cook or be domestic in any way. The table was set to perfection. Each dish was placed just so in order to make it easy to sample the tempting foods. It was quite a sight to behold. As the family took their seats for the Christmas feast in the early evening after saying grace, while giving herself a pep talk beforehand, Willow mustered the courage to speak and decided to keep it simple, opening up the discussion with a question.

"I've been putting some thought into what I would like to do for my senior project. What do y'all think about my forming a band of young people from around the world who are committed to working together to protect and clean up the planet?"

Betsy replied, "Whatever gave you an idea such as

that? Surely, you don't mean to leave home to do this project, right? You've never been away from here or out of the state before. I can't imagine what you're thinking, dear."

"I know, Mother, but I want to continue my environmental studies and activism. Going out into the world will allow me to do that. Don't you understand?"

Daniel spoke in a consoling tone, "I think it's a great idea, Willow, dear. Your grades are excellent. Good enough for you to do anything you want. I think your teacher, Ms. Norris, would be willing to listen to your ideas and give you her honest opinion and some helpful suggestions too."

Betsy's voice was noticeably strained, "Yes, but what she wants to do sounds dangerous, Daniel!"

Looking at her while winking with a broad, effusive smile, Paul chimed in, "Aw, she'll be alright, Ma. You guys are always praising her for everything: she's at the top of her class, spends all of her spare time as a volunteer with Kentucky First and is the best daughter and sister anyone could ever hope for. I think we can trust her to figure things out for herself."

"I agree with Paul," Daniel added. "Willow has sound values and good boundaries. I trust her completely to make the right decisions. From what I've seen, she can accomplish anything she sets her mind to."

Betsy sat back in her chair. A look of resignation appeared as she let out a heavy sigh. While focusing her attention squarely on her daughter, she replied: "Oh well, once again, I've been outvoted. I guess I'm just an old worry wart. I believe in you too, dear. I just don't want to see you get hurt or lose you."

"Don't worry. I won't get hurt and you will absolutely never lose me, dear Mother. Anyway, it's still just an idea. I have to work out all the details before taking any action. I wanted to hear what you guys thought first. That's all."

Willow stared fondly into the familiar faces assembled before her. In an instant, she felt how lucky she was to have grown up with so much love. At this moment, she grasped how vital the work of attempting to save our fragile planet was. The realization gave her a sense of pride. She knew what a benefit it was to have had that kind of solid upbringing and she also knew she could always lean on her family for support. This assurance empowered her and the cause, as well.

Willow got choked up and emotional. As the tears welled up in her eyes, she said, "You mean so much to me. I'm proud to call myself an O'Brien. Everything I've done over the years, each accomplishment at school and in my personal life, comes down to all of you being there for me. The belief in myself is due to this family. It's what makes me want to be a better person and put forth the effort to follow a higher purpose. Your faith makes me feel like I can do anything."

After dinner, the group made merry. They assembled around the tree to exchange gifts, taking turns opening presents.

Daniel softly tapped his daughter's shoulder, holding

in the palm of his hand a neatly wrapped gift. "Here, sweetie. This is for you."

Willow was barely able to wait until the time came for her to open the present.

As she unwrapped the small box and removed its top, she found an odd-shaped object inside that resembled a watch. "Oh, daddy!" she said with delight.

"It's a compass, dear one. You love nature so much that I thought it would come in handy so you'd never get lost while out exploring. Now though, after tonight, I think it will help you to always find your way back home…to us."

Just as she'd done so long ago, she reached up and hugged her father around the neck, whispering in his ear, "I love it, and you too, Daddy."

As the night's revelries and celebration wound down, everyone said their "good nights" while heading toward the comfort of a warm bed and the pleasure of a peaceful night's sleep. It was going to be hard, but necessary, for Willow to put the earlier events of the day into perspective. If her parents agreed to let her go and her teacher approved the plan that allowed her to be away, it may be possible to fulfill The Oracle's request. However, what were the actual steps that she needed to take? This was all so new. Her heart was telling her one thing, but her head stayed stuck in the details. Only confusion remained.

Willow tried to relax so that she could fall asleep, knowing that the grand plan would still be there in the morning. As she began to nod off, she became aware of an energetic presence. In an instant, there was a wave of tingling sensations all over her body. This would be the first time, but not the last, that she would experience this feeling. Willow sat upright in bed as the apparition materialized before her. It was the same figure dressed all in white, her hair was richly adorned with brown and green foliage, braided throughout with the colors of nature. “Is it you, Mother?” Willow inquired.

“Yes, dear, it is. I’ll come when you need me, in times of doubt, struggling to find answers. This will always be the way between us. You will never feel alone.”

It was strange becoming accustomed to communicating with an ethereal spirit. However, she thought it felt deeply reassuring.

“I’m in need, Mother. I don’t know where to begin this journey. I don’t know what to do. You seem to have faith in me, but I have none in myself.”

“Over time, as you grow stronger and gain more confidence in becoming a great leader, you will seek out my help less and less. This is hard to believe now. What are you confused about, my dear?”

Willow furrowed her brow as she asked, “Where am I to start? The only people I know are from here. I don’t know anyone else from the outside world. I spoke to my folks tonight and they agreed to support me in whatever plans I want to pursue. They really are the greatest…I’m so grateful to have them. As much as I trust my family, I dare not share the experiences I’ve had with you, Mother.”

Looking at her as a parent would look at her own child, Mother replied, "You're not alone. There are many people who are sympathetic to our cause. I'll reach out and communicate with them telepathically so that they're aware you're seeking their services and in need of help. The journey you've embarked on is a spiritual one that many won't understand. It's a leap of faith into the unknown that I'll assist you in taking."

Willow pinched herself to make sure that she wasn't dreaming.

She wasn't.

The Oracle continued, "Now, tell me…what else is troubling you, my dear?"

Before speaking, she buoyed herself: "You'd said you wanted me to form a group of like-minded youth. Who are these youth and where will I find them?"

The benevolent spirit slowly began to fade, drifting out of view. While departing, she spoke in a clear voice saying, "This is a question you will have to answer for yourself. Search your heart and listen to your intuition. That is where you'll find what you're looking for."

Willow was bewildered. She sat on the edge of her bed and was unable to speak. The energetic signature of the ethereal presence was palpable and lingered in the room. What was happening to her? It was as if she'd been struck by a bolt of lightning that day and was forever changed by the experience. Somehow, through it all, a reassuring sense of calm remained. In a moment of clarity, Willow realized a big truth. Mother's words would be deeply imprinted into her subconscious. They would serve as a guide. All that was left was to look for the signs and the path Mother had laid out. She dropped off into a tranquil sleep. Hoping that, by morning, the fantasy would match the reality and provide her with greater clarity.

Willow met with her teacher, Ms. Norris, on the break. It was a common practice to have a meeting in order to discuss ideas about a proposal for a senior project. Once the student presented a plan, the teacher could provide recommendations.

"Your parents called and told me you wanted to focus on environmental activism as your career goal and had an idea for the senior project. Is that right?"

"Oh, yes, Ms. Norris. You're well aware I have been involved as a volunteer with Kentucky First for some time now. I feel my education would benefit from being away from home and learning about the impact of pollution on different world environments. Also, I believe there are other young people, like me, who want to make a difference. I want to see whether we can put a group together; this group would provide protection and restore the health of the planet in any way we can."

"That is quite an ambitious undertaking. How will you be able to finance such an enterprise? It could be quite expensive, you know", her teacher said while listening in rapt attention to Willow speak.

"Actually, I haven't a clue. Maybe, there are environmental organizations that can help fund such a project."

"From what I know of nonprofits, they usually ask

the public to finance their activities. They most likely don't have the resources to contribute."

"At this point, Ms. Norris, I don't know how I can make this come together. I still believe there is a solution out there somewhere,"Willow said optimistically.

"After you work out those important details, let's get back together and revisit your idea. I'm here for you if you need me, okay?"

"Yes, I will," she said. Willow thanked her teacher and waved goodbye deciding to bravely forge ahead by taking the initial step on the journey, knowing that no obstacles could deter her. Still though, she waited anxiously over the last week of winter break to get word from those individuals Mother had mentioned who were sympathetic to the cause, hoping they would reach out to her soon. Who were they? How would they know how to contact her? What would they bring in the way of help and support? These were burning questions that were impossible to answer. She kept the worrying down to a minimum and held a vigil in silence.

At the tail end of her break and just before New Year's Day, Willow heard the phone ringing downstairs. Paul was in the den. He was watching a football game when the call came in.

Standing at the bottom of the stairs, he hollered, "It's for you!" Suggesting she take it in their their parents' room.

"Willow inquired, "Who is it, Paul?"

"I don't know. Sis. Some older guy. He didn't say."

"Okay, no big deal…I'll find out who it is."

Willow wandered into her parents' bedroom and picked up the phone. "Hello", she replied in a cheery voice. "Who am I speaking to?"

"Hi, my name is Sam Teyer. Sorry, but for the life of me, I don't remember how I got this number and why I'm calling. Who are you?"

"My name is Willow O'Brien."

"That doesn't ring a bell," he replied. Tell me a little bit about yourself."

A peaceful calm spread over her entire body as she spoke. "Okay. I'm seventeen years old and a senior in high school. I'm passionately devoted to environmental activism. That's all I can think about day and night. Who are you, sir?"

"Well. young lady, I'm the CEO of a large investment corporation. Our prime concern involves the preservation of the natural world."

Willow knew intuitively that this man was the one Mother Earth had communicated with telepathically. He had been sent to provide the help she needed to carry out the mission.

"That sounds wonderful! I have an idea we were destined to meet."

Sam paused thoughtfully before speaking, "Hmmm, yes. I have a strange feeling, too, that some kind of divine intervention brought us together. I don't know how, but I think I know why. How can I help you, my dear?"

Willow breathed a huge sigh of relief. "I'm committed to forming a group of young environmental activists from around the world who oppose individuals or corporations that are involved in destroying the earth."

"It sounds like those individuals and corporations you're talking about are what we in this business call Disturbers," he pointed out. "Their activities account for 70% of global emissions and are the chief cause of the damage to the planet. For some time now, I've felt that the youth movement would be the key to our success in stemming this destructive tide. I don't know why we were brought together, but far be it for me to question the workings of the Universe."

"I'm young and have no money. All I possess is my desire to do this with all my heart and soul. Will you help me?" she pleaded.

"I'm a businessman. Very seldom do I make important decisions by following my heart and not my head. However, this time may be different. From what you've told me, your mission meets the criteria we've established for investing in environmental projects. Even though you're quite a bit younger than others we have funded, I believe your group might be an excellent addition and a great asset to restoring the planet. So, my answer is yes. I'll back you financially in any way I can. Our attorney, Peter Kensington, will be at your disposal to assist you along the way."

"Really? You mean it? That is unbelievably good news. Thank you, Sam!" Willow replied joyfully. "Now, I can take the necessary steps to form a group. With your help, I'll be able to be away from home to do it."

"Have you given any thought as to what you want to name the group?"

"Over these last weeks, I have considered that question, but I can't find a good one that fits," she said with enthusiasm.

"May I make a suggestion? From what you've told me about your passion and willingness to protect the environment, it reminds me of an eco-warrior. An eco-warrior is committed to the cause and stands up for justice right to the bitter end."

She stood still in complete amazement. Could this really be true? The wishes of The Oracle were coming to pass right before her eyes and she was a part of making it happen?! It was almost too much to believe.

"You have given me such a gift today, Sam. I'll take your suggestion and call our group The Warriors."

"From here on out, young lady, I dub this group Willow's Warriors and you as its leader."

She blushed shyly upon hearing the name and then said, "I'll do my very best to always live up to its mission and strive to make the world a better place."

"I have all the confidence that you will." He said as he encouraged her to reach out to him as the need arises, bidding fond farewell until the next time.

Chapter 3

Willow's Romance

"A first love is the soul's purest kiss." – Angie Weiland-Crosby

After meeting Mother Earth, Willow felt a strong urge to create a group of like-minded people. She started the movement by searching for dedicated people on different social media platforms and posing them a simple question: "Who loves the planet enough to save it?" She got hundreds of replies. But only a few of them were sincere and real enough to be worthy of joining the group. To ascertain who was thoroughly dedicated to the movement, Willow set up interviews to meet each of the interested parties in order to discuss their backgrounds. She met a small band of young men called the Anti-Fractivists. They consisted of three: Julian from Canada, Donald from Michigan and Rowdy from Texas. All of them are budding activists in the environmental movement.

The Anti-Fracks actively protested organizations in the oil industry. They stood up to the corrupt system, opposing the practice of fracking in their home states as a way of protecting the natural environment. Fracking, an unpleasant process, involves drilling into the strata and substrata of the earth in order to extract fossil fuels. It is a vile method that causes geologic plate movement, destabilization, and earthquakes. This practice is the oil industry's last attempt to take anything that remains, simultaneously exerting its power and control over the populace through an insatiable dependence on fossil fuels, regardless of the many negative and detrimental environmental effects.

Willow never forgot the day she first met the Anti-Fracks and Rowdy. She was particularly on edge and distressed for some unknown reason. There was an uncomfortable tug at her insides, and this made her feel uneasy. Something was in the wind, like an unusual aspect that hung heavy in the air. She couldn't predict what was about to happen exactly. The feeling was very odd and unsettling. Willow steadied herself and gained composure by focusing on the purpose of the mission and the cause. The message of protection, renewal and survival for all sentient beings served as a meditation and provided a grounding influence to balance her mood. Knowing what her purpose was, imbued in her a profound dedication which was combined with the spirit of unwavering resolve to never forget the highest good no matter what the challenges were.

The meeting was scheduled to take place at Willow's family home. She grew up there. It was familiar. It was a safe haven of comfort and, most of all, love. It nurtured a deep appreciation of the natural world, as well as a sense of belonging and where real beauty and peace could be found. All of the sights, sounds and smells were reminders that pleasantly colored fond memories of her youth.

Willow glanced at the clock. It was around 12:45 pm. The meeting was scheduled for 1:00 pm. She peered out the living room window and looked intently for any sign they were coming. Off in the distance and up the road a piece, the persistent loud honking of a car horn could be heard. A few minutes later, she saw an old, dented Chevy Tahoe kicking up a cloud of dust as it made its way toward her residence.

When Betsy, Willow's mom, heard the commotion while taking her daily nap, she came into view at the top of the stairs to see what was going on. Ginger, the family dog, followed closely behind. She was a red Queensland and Willow's pet. They were inseparable companions and faithful explorers across the wilds of Kentucky. She enjoyed those regular romps just as much as Willow did.

Betsy yawned, looking slightly drowsy and was not yet fully awake, "Are those your friends, dear...the ones you were expecting?"

"Yes, I think so, Mom. I hope they won't bother you. We'll just be in the living room, ok?"

"You go right ahead, dear, and have a nice visit. Let me know if you need anything, ok?" Turning around slowly, she headed off in the direction of the kitchen to get preparations for the evenings' meal started. Ginger toddled along behind eager to find out what was for dinner.

Accompanied by lots of clatter and loud engine noise, the old truck pulled into the yard and came to an abrupt halt. Willow stifled the urge to put on her best manners and display her southern charm right away. She wanted to get a better look, but preferred to wait until they came up to the door. She watched closely as they got out of the truck, one by one. First, there was the tall guy with long blond hair tied back in a neat ponytail, wearing Aviator-type sunglasses. Arching his back to stretch and to show off his physique, he appeared to be on the serious side. Willow felt sure he was the leader of the group. He had a confident, demeanor and commanded attention. Next, there came a well-built, dark-complected, good-looking type who was short, stocky and compact. Seeming to be a pleasant fellow with an easy-going way about him, he was smiling broadly as he got out of the truck.

Willow wondered who was driving. Blinking to clear her vision, she peered hard at the young man about medium height who stepped down. He had shoulder-length curly hair. It was loosely unkempt and wild. His red hair, vivid red at that, had a glow about it in the midday sun. Mesmerized, she couldn't take her eyes off him. Unable to direct her gaze elsewhere, she thought,

'What's the matter with me? My heart is racing. I must get hold of myself.' Just as quickly as they arrived, the energetic men marched up the steps together and straight onto the porch knocking loudly. Willow was reserved as she answered the door. The first to greet her was the tall blond with a serious, but friendly expression.

He spoke in a very matter-of-fact tone and smiled from ear to ear, "Hi, my name is Julian. I'm from Canada."

Right behind him was the good-looking one who seemed kind of shy. He immediately stuck out his hand to introduce himself, "Nice to meet you. My name is Donald. I'm from Michigan."

"Very nice to meet you too. Please come right in." Willow greeted them both with all the cordiality she had been taught as a good southern girl. With a polite wave of her hand, she ushered the two forward and gestured them to come in.

Last, but not least, was the redhead. He looked unpredictable and rambunctious, but when Willow gazed into his soulful eyes, she couldn't help staring. They were a teal blue with hints of green, so vibrant they captivated her completely. Willow stuttered nervously as she spoke, "Wel... Welcome...you, you must be Rowdy."

Without speaking, he nodded in the affirmative. Then in a subtle Texas drawl, he replied, "and you must be Willow." Tilting his head slyly to one side as he smiled. Willow blushed. Her face turned a remarkable shade of red, matching the color of his hair, while beckoning him to enter.

Still a little shaken by his presence, she thought, *What's the matter with me? He's just a boy around my age. Nothing out of the ordinary. Why am I so nervous?* Still, she couldn't help feeling awe-struck. There was a familiarity about him that transcended the typical first encounter one has when meeting somebody new. It was uncanny. Julian and Donald noticed the sparks flying between them, but the guys remained silent and respectful of their hostess. They were genuinely shocked and amazed by what they were witnessing.

The meeting went well. They shared their life stories with Willow. Julian spoke about how in some Canadian provinces they allow the practice of fracking, while others ban it. The process involves massive amounts of water, which is used to release oil and natural gas deposits that were previously inaccessible. Julian made it clear that when water is combined with chemicals and sand, it becomes toxic. Once used and contaminated it must be disposed of somehow. This affects the groundwater in a harmful way. Pollution results and the drilling creates geologic instability.

Rowdy spoke of his early childhood. He grew up with a father who was a roughneck in the Texas oil industry. He saw very little of his dad as a young boy, since he worked long hours on a job that involved doing dangerous, life-threatening activities. He was a hard-working, hard-living, coarse, heavy-drinking man, who was not patient and often physically and verbally abusive to his mom. Those early childhood experiences were stressful and influenced his impression of the industry in a negative way. In his mind, the blight on the landscape from oil derricks was damaging to the natural world as well. It was clear to Willow, from what she'd heard, that Rowdy had been affected, as she had, by an exploitative industry that was greedily bent on harvesting natural resources. Donald's experience wasn't much different. He was from Michigan, a state known for its fracking industry. His experience was one similar to the others that affected the social and environmental landscape as well. Willow also asked them to talk about the kind of strategies they would employ when confronting Disturbers forces.

Rowdy responded first. He was outspoken and confident. "We would react to them in the least violent way possible. Our approach has always been to confound and confuse them with the truth. This is something they're not used to. It's clear they manipulate the system to get what they want. They buy politicians as they go. They allow DF's to operate their refineries without any controls, so they can continue to pollute the environment. Our main strategy is to get people to strike and protest, which is their civic duty and right as concerned citizens. Otherwise, muted and silent, their voices can't be heard."

Willow wondered if it were obvious to Rowdy how he'd impressed her. She was proud to be a part of this great mission when she heard him speak. After listening to each of them share their experiences as environmental activists, she knew these men were solid and Warrior material who must become part of the group. They were young, committed and each had a good character with the solid morals, values and ideals necessary for a higher purpose. Willow explained to the guys that she was beginning to create The Warriors and wanted to connect with all interested parties before she finished choosing the members. She bade them farewell, for the time being, with the assurance they would be contacted again soon.

Later that night, Willow looked up into the star-filled sky while she was standing on the front porch. The same sense of uneasiness she'd had earlier came over her again. She prided herself on being able to handle anything, no matter what the situation. However, there was still a sense of discomfort that lingered. Her personal philosophy was: *Always find the balance...it's in all things.* It was strange, though, but she couldn't get the image of Rowdy out of her mind. As Willow contemplated her feelings, she felt a powerful wave of vibrational energy come over her. At that very moment, the presence of The Oracle, Mother Earth, materialized. Willow was startled and a bit surprised. "But Mother, I didn't call for you."

The Oracle replied, "I'm never very far away from you, my dear. I exist in the trees, the water and the stars in the sky. I always know when you need me, Willow."

"Oh, Mother, you're so right! I feel very unsure of myself. I want to be strong, but at this moment, I'm as weak and fragile as a newborn kitten. I need to remain true in my heart and not get distracted by emotions that take away from the cause and staying focused."

"Then what is it you're afraid of, Willow?" asked The Oracle.

"I don't know, Mother. When I looked into the eyes of that young man today, I felt my heart race and my pulse pound. I had trouble breathing and couldn't catch my breath to speak. I was so nervous and I was shaking all over. It made me very uncomfortable. I just know that he must be someone special, because I saw in his face and listened to him talk about the importance to prioritize the needs of others before ever thinking of himself. He was also very familiar to me somehow."

Mother spoke, replying calmly, "You have experienced what's called soul recognition that has made you more spiritually aware. You've met someone with whom you have a deep bond and connection with. This is a person whose energy and enthusiasm match your own. In truth, it is a rare and beautiful gift. Rowdy is on the same ascended path as you. You're both mutually linked on this journey. The strength you two have will be a powerful force in this struggle. It has been created to defeat the evil that threatens to destroy the planet. Since you care for each other so much, your divine love will guide you."

Just as Willow was forming the words to ask Mother another question, she vanished as suddenly and unexpectedly as she'd appeared. While Willow was pondering what to say, a strong, reassuring calm swept over her. It was a liberating force. The message was clear and profound. Every living being was part of a larger integrated whole. Each being was seamlessly flowing and interdependent upon the other. Nature was in perfect harmony, while humans were disconnected and out of sync with everything around them. It would be up to her and other like-minded youth, such as Rowdy and the rest, to collectively clean up the planet and save the Earth. The knowledge was a powerful revelation, and it came as a great blessing.

That night, with Ginger sleeping comfortably at the foot of her bed, Willow gave thanks and prayed for those she loved to be safe. The whirlwind events of the day made perfect sense at last. All doubts were removed and replaced by a great sense of duty and responsibility. Willow felt her heart surge with joy and pride, hardly able to contain herself. She knew full well that this awareness would help to guide The Warriors forward as she directed the actions of the group in the days and months to come. She wondered silently if she would be strong enough to lead. The reassuring response always came from a familiar calming voice, “Yes, my dear...you are.” Willow breathed in and exhaled a long sigh of relief as she fell into a deep, peaceful sleep she hadn't felt since childhood.

As time went on, after their first meeting at the O’Brien home, Willow started to feel a palpable urge that invaded her energy. This strange, unexplainable longing was accompanied by a rush of pure excitement at the thought of closeness and of having Rowdy’s arms wrapped tightly around her. She imagined those arms to be protective in their strength, bordering on perfection and providing a soothing comfort from frequent stress and doubt. Rowdy enlivened all of her senses, moving her spiritually in ways she’d never experienced before.

The feelings were so real. She knew they had to be true. That bond of intimacy was no minor coincidence. It was impossible to brush aside lightly. Privately, she would fantasize about his long, slender fingers, tan in color and dotted liberally with freckles, reaching out to caress her face in a sweetly soft and gentle way. The desire to surrender completely quickly replaced any notion of resistance. It was much more than a physical attraction. Willow knew she was connected to Rowdy spiritually and, most especially, through her heart. As their relationship grew, their spiritual connection was clearly becoming deeper with each passing day.

Alone together on those special occasions, discussing plans for the Warriors, Willow felt a warm, calming sensation. It invaded her consciousness while evoking many soft, feminine feelings of vulnerability in his masculine presence. She was afraid he would sense the enormity of her affection and run away, so she tried to suppress that passionate energy. As she was developing into a young woman and physically maturing, forbidden thoughts of surrendering to Rowdy occurred with greater frequency. Tender acts of romantic love crossed her mind on a regular basis and interfered at times with her attempt to maintain focus on the higher purpose. In the midst of this, however, a deep, abiding trust and devotion to one another remained; it was a closeness that transcended their age and naïveté. It felt so pure and natural and was beautifully expressed. It was like a rose in full bloom that was awash in sunlight thirsty to be nurtured. The presence of a strong, spiritual bond magnetized their connection which was a mirror that reflected their infinite love for the planet. Their love was in sync with the natural world. It shone bright around people, as it fostered a dying planet and shepherded it through renewal for future generations.

She knew as their relationship progressed, being physically close seemed inevitable. Willow had never had a boyfriend, although she felt instinctively Rowdy would be the perfect choice. Not only did she have a great deal of respect for him, as he was sincere, honest and gentle, but because he also followed the same spiritual path she did. In Willow's eyes, this made him divine. She knew when the time was right, he would share his mind, body and soul with her completely.

It was understood by all that Willow's position, as head of The Warriors, was one of leadership. Mother Earth, The Oracle, through her contributions of benevolence, knowledge, compassion and divine intervention, would guide in the decision-making. The activities, engagements and responses toward Disturber forces were made collectively. Each member had an equal say. Rowdy never attempted to undermine Willow's authority and gave her the utmost respect at all times. By disciplining herself, she made a solemn vow to uphold the highest ideals and took full responsibility for any decisions or actions. Ultimately, the cause of protecting and preserving the planet would take precedence over any personal interests or desires; that included her love for Rowdy.

As was her way, Willow pondered whether she would

be able to do the important work of organizing that her activism required. Her responsibilities were steadily mounting and their activities garnered a growing notoriety worldwide. Each event, including meeting Rowdy, had moved the cause forward and into the spotlight. She wondered, with so much happening, would Rowdy be someone she could trust to be there when things got difficult?

Willow worried about her feelings for Rowdy. She was troubled by the thought that her growing fondness for him might start to become apparent. This was nerve-wracking. It wouldn't be easy keeping romantic thoughts private when they were spending so much time getting to know one another. However, with the business at hand, it was important to keep a clear head. She felt as if she was adrift in uncharted waters. These waters were exciting and waiting to be explored, but at another time and place. Willow viewed Rowdy as a man of deliberate action. He put himself in harm's way and stood up for the environment. He was wild and impetuous. Although he had a reckless nature, his boundless energy, courage and integrity made him an invaluable asset to the group.

The night in Poland after the Climate Accords, while sharing a chamomile tea and croissant, he confessed, "I hope you know how much you mean to me." He smiled lovingly and lightly touched her hand as he spoke. At the time, Willow was unsure and unable to fully accept their unique connection. She spoke frankly and said, "If you love me, then you'll never leave me, but if you don't...you will." It seemed a pretty simple choice in a naive sort of way. She knew he was aligned with her politics and beliefs, but was his admiration a good thing in the face of the mounting demands of the movement, or was it more of a diversion and a pleasant distraction that might not go too well with the higher purpose of the mission? Only time would tell.

On another occasion, as their romance blossomed, the Anti-Fracks stayed busy along the Gulf Coast of Texas, devising new and interesting ways to upend the twisted oil industry to ultimately throw a monkey wrench into hostile forces' diabolical plans to exploit the natural world for profit. Willow's mind drifted as she thought of tilting at windmills, wondering whether one of her favorite characters, Don Quixote, ever considered climate change in his lifetime. Questions formed in her mind. Did wind power cause cancer? Were they a blight on the landscape like so many thought, or did it reflect more on the common human tendency to see things superficially as healthy when nothing could be further from the truth? People didn't want to acknowledge the problem, even when it was staring them straight in the face and they were fully aware of the disintegrating environment around them. Willow was sure it was a visual cortex thing and a processing glitch in the collective consciousness. Hopefully, it was open to revision.

This kind of thinking seemed absurd in the moment, though, especially with the survival of the planet, air, water, land and the animals dangling in the balance. The exponential rise of natural disasters around the world, which were occurring with greater frequency, threatened to change the Earth forever. The daily extinction of animal species taking place at an accelerated rate made the future look bleak. Willow's generation would not be seeing the living world like it is now, but would experience it as virtual reality in the very near future. This outcome was certain if conditions continued as they were. While she was thinking back, Willow remembered something Rowdy said that she'd forgotten along the way. It brought her clarity and put everything into perspective.

Taking as deep a breath as possible, Willow let out a long sigh, "I wish I could breathe better...it really isn't the way it used to be years ago when I was a young girl." She was thinking and talking aloud as she stood and stared out the window. Just then, she heard footsteps coming toward her.

Rowdy entered the room, huffing and puffing, "Hey, Willow, you gonna just stand around all day when we've got so much work to do? Say...what goes on here?"

Willow turned to greet him with a sad expression on her face, "Hey, I was just thinking about how things are so bad out there and wondering to myself if we're making any difference at all."

Rowdy wrapped his arms around her in a comforting and consoling way. "You're my hero. I wouldn't be here if it weren't for you! For me and the rest of the guys, we'd follow you anywhere!" he said, planting a tender kiss on her forehead.

Willow smiled while looking into his sea-green eyes as she acknowledged his sweet words. "As long as we stay together, we stay strong! Like Mother Earth said, “We Exist!" Confirming what they both knew with a confident certainty that the journey was just beginning and there was much to do, they clasped hands firmly going out to join the others.

Chapter 4

Oceana's Adventure

"Far and away, the greatest threat to the ocean, and thus to ourselves, is ignorance. But, we can do something about that." - Sylvia Earle

Bill was a local fisherman who made a modest living angling for striped bass to sell to local restaurants in Providence, Newport and Fall River communities. Two seasons ago, he was trolling near home waters in Narragansett Bay off the coast of Rhode Island. It was a particularly warm July morning. Bill felt an unusually strong pull on his line. He thought, "I must have a really big one on... it feels like I'm in for quite a fight!" Carefully reeling in his catch, he started to see what looked like the face of a girl! As he pondered what it might be, he said to himself, "Am I dreamin'? Is that what I think it is? She looks human! These waters are so freezing cold.

How could anyone survive those frigid temperatures?" Bill slowed the boat down to a crawl so he could get a better look. As he continued reeling, an unidentifiable life form came into view. What could that be? Yes, it was! A mermaid and a blond one to boot!

Rising to the surface of the water, her body floated limp and lifeless as it drifted alongside the boat. At that moment, Bill thought back to ancient tales of mermaid sightings that crusty, old mariners told while looking for drinks at the local bar. He knew these wild, far-fetched stories were just alcohol-induced fantasies. Bill had done a bit of drinking himself in his younger years, but he could always tell the difference between truth and fiction. Gone were the days when he believed the rumors. He was all about writing off those legends as wild ramblings as he now preferred hard facts to fairy tales. When he heard of mermaids swimming up from hidden depths at the bottom of the ocean, those tales were honestly too unbelievable to be true.

After careful consideration, Bill decided to rig up a hoist and bring her on board. Getting a sling under her petite frame didn't require a great deal of effort, since her condition was weakened. As he got into the right position to bring her on board, his hands ever so slightly in the water, a small sea creature swam up and rammed its body into one of Bill's fingers. "Ow!" He let out a yelp while looking over the water to locate what attacked him. With a force of determination, much mightier than its size, a Hippocampus raced by the side of the boat and wedged itself in-between Bill and the resting mermaid.

Quite by surprise, he found himself trying to talk to the protective seahorse.

"Hey, little fella...what's the problem?' Is she a friend of yours? I know...I'll get her some coconut water." He shrugged his shoulders as he walked away and scratched his head, unsure if she even drank coconut water.

Hurrying to the galley, Bill grabbed what he needed and returned to provide aid and comfort. Her little protector backed off to give him some room to operate. With a sudden start, the semi-conscious mermaid bolted upright. Dazed, she stared straight into Bill's eyes. With one swift move, she arched her back fully to gain thrust and vaulted forward off the bow, landing with a loud splash. He didn't try to stop her. Bill was stunned as he silently watched her swim away. Moving slowly, still weakened by the experience with the little seahorse in tow, wondering at that moment if he'd ever see her again.

Within weeks of their first meeting, the answer came. While he was trolling the Bay, he glimpsed a shimmering object in the water. As it moved within a few yards of the boat, the familiar face of the young mermaid appeared. This time, she wore a smile and acted as if she was eager to make his acquaintance.

He waved and returned her friendly greeting, "Hi, there. Where's your little friend?"

Oceana pointed toward the stern of the boat where the reluctant seahorse hid out.

"Hey, little fella...what 'ya' afraid of? I don't bite!" Bill laughed heartily.

Zippy bristled defensively and slowly swam over to

where Oceana was treading water. He reacted like a loyal dog when strangers were around and was overly protective of his mistress. Bill bent down to the railing of the boat to speak. Shaking her head from side to side, Oceana indicated she was unable to communicate verbally.

He thought: *Hmm, I'm gonna have to devise a way for us to talk, but what can I do?*

Rustling up a pencil and paper, he drew a rough sketch of her and pointed to it. "What's your name? Who are you?" She looked confused at first but then nodded that she understood what he was asking.

Bill gazed out beyond the Bay and stared across the deep blue ocean. Waves were rising, falling and crashing against the distant shore.

He looked back down at her and said, "Since you came here from the depths of the sea, I'll call you...Oceana... and your salty little friend... Zippy."

Bill's life was a humble one. He was in his late 50s and had been a widower for many years. He was used to living alone on a houseboat in the local harbor. A simple, uncomplicated man, he was quiet, pleasant and well-liked in the community. Making a modest living that adequately met his needs, he managed quite well on the earnings of a fisherman. Bill's daily routine consisted of rising early in the morning, with his strong coffee in hand, as he made sure the boat was rigged right and fully stocked with fishing supplies, lures, line and food for the day. As much as he enjoyed his life, it seemed there was always something missing. A sort of melancholy, especially in the evenings, would come upon him from time to time. That sadness would subside at first light, though, as he rose to get the day started.

After meeting Oceana and Zippy, a new sensation of wonder and enchantment replaced the sadness. He started to look at the connection as the means to examine his own life, thinking a good deal about the well-being of his newfound friends and what this chance meeting meant. He pondered how he might ask whether they would like to live with him and come home to a place of safety and comfort where they'd always be welcome.

It wouldn't be long before Bill got the opening he was looking for. As the temperature began to turn cold and winter was settling in upon the Northeast, he spent most of his time staying in the harbor and keeping warm in an imposed hibernation until spring. Early one Sunday morning, while taking a leisurely stroll around the deck of his houseboat, a small, white and brown-speckled seahorse appeared at the aft of the vessel. It was Zippy. He was gyrating, back and forth, in panic mode, along the length of the moored ship.

"Hi there, say…what's the matter, little fella?" Zippy sped in the direction of the harbor entrance and then back to Bill. "Is it Oceana? Where is she?" Without hesitation, Bill hopped aboard his fishing boat and headed out. He followed the tiny wake of the little seahorse as he propelled himself forward.

Bill navigated to a place known as Hazard Rock, which was off in the distance. There, Oceana lay sprawled out. Her hair was whipped across her face in a tangled mess. She was balled up in a contorted position and clutching at her stomach. Bill drove the boat in closer, careful not to run aground. He shouted, "I'm here to help you!" The nervous seahorse whirled in circles and sped around in hyperdrive.

Bill anchored near the base of the rock at the calmest place possible. After checking out the situation, he noticed half-eaten clam shells strewn around. Some of their contents were missing. Bill knelt down close and asked, as he pointed to the shells, "Did you eat these?" She nodded her head, yes. He knew that at certain times of the year, the consumption of shellfish out of season would cause a form of physical paralysis. It's a temporary, but very real and deadly condition. She was showing all the signs of food poisoning. Bill attributed this as the most likely cause of her illness. It seemed pretty clear that he would have to intervene again, this time to save her life.

Since Oceana was in a fragile state, he moved her with great care and managed to transfer her onto the vessel with very little difficulty. They returned to the houseboat where he could tend to her properly. He paid special attention to the delicate condition and made sure it didn't get worse.

In the days that followed, Bill nursed Oceana back to health with seaweed broth and barley tea; this was a healing regimen for cleansing the system. Bill summoned the courage to ask, as tactfully as possible, if she would like to come to live with him or at least consider his houseboat home when she was traveling through these waters.

One peaceful day, while she was drinking the healthful broth and recuperating, Bill softly suggested, "Since you and Zippy don't have a permanent home, would you like to stay here with me?" A look of deep concern appeared on his face.

He drew a picture of her with Zippy; they were both resting comfortably in a cabin on the boat.

"Especially during the winter months when it's too cold to be out there traveling...you would be welcome here."

Oceana looked kindly at Bill and glanced out through the porthole, which was facing back out to sea. She paused for a moment. With half a smile, she shyly nodded her head up and down to indicate yes. Bill exhaled a sigh of relief. He looked fondly at the young mermaid, who was timid yet strong in her determination to survive. He intuitively felt their chance meeting was no accident. He was going to embark on a great adventure and one he would soon discover was the highest purpose anyone could have… saving the Earth. At the same time, he would be doing a good deed for Oceana and Zippy too. They would be able to call this their new home.

Bill devised a way for Oceana to have a berth in a compartment. It was a cargo hold for cold storage originally used to keep fish fresh. It was located below the deck. There was a hatch that could be unlatched from the inside.

Oceana could slide in and out to moisturize and refresh her scaly skin and tail. The system worked well. It was the ideal solution. She could stay on the boat in comfort and have ease of movement with the least amount of exposure to the outside world. Bill would often stand watch on deck as she swam alone in the Bay. Zippy hung out close by. He was sheltered within the harbor and careful to avoid being seen. Oceana made lazy circles in the water for exercise and relaxation. With one swish of her broad tail, she dove deep to the bottom and settled into a comfortable position. Her muscular tail wrapped around cocoon-like and created an outer shell for protection. She was extremely shy, and somewhat frightened of humans. Privacy was much needed. With great pride, Bill relished the role of protector and appreciated the company of his newfound friends.

Oceana presented with a variety of challenges, but she managed to live through them. She possessed silver, blond tresses, sparkling blue eyes and attracted attention from many sources. These assets made her an easy target in open waters. There were times when Oceana narrowly escaped disaster. Bill rescued her once by distracting a hungry tiger shark. He lured it away by using live bait. Another time, a sport fisherman, thinking he had a gilt-colored marlin on his line, accidentally hooked her broad tail. Freeing herself, she pulled the hook out by hand and quickly escaped back to the safety of the sea. On another occasion, the flash of her shimmering metallic color attracted an amorous blue whale during the mating season along the Mendocino coast. Luckily, that time, she managed to outmaneuver the enormous suitor, using her quickness and agility. It was this type of scenario that Bill was all too familiar with, as he remembered coming into contact with her in a similar way.

Shortly after they moved in, Bill was scrolling through the internet on the computer, checking his email early one evening. He observed a post that grabbed his attention.

The one-line post read, "Who loves the planet enough to save it?" The comment included the person's name, Willow O'Brien, and her email address.

Bill wondered to himself: *Is Oceana here for some unknown reason? From wherever she came, she may be searching for someone and it might be this Willow person.* Bill felt it was his duty to find out. He made up his mind right then and there to make contact with Willow that night. He communicated in the most subtle terms possible with the least amount of detail. He didn't want to surprise or shock her, when he mentioned his friend was a mermaid. Bill didn't have long to wait to receive a response. By the next morning, he got a reply.

Willow naturally showed a great deal of curiosity about Oceana. She immediately made plans to drive up to Rhode Island from Kentucky as soon as possible to meet them both. Willow could hardly believe what good fortune it would be to have someone like Oceana, an aquatic activist, on the team. The possibilities were endless!

When Willow left that night, the moon was shining down upon her. Optimistic, her sense of hope fueled the ten-hour drive. When she reached her destination on the

Bay, she was eager to get to work. She easily found the houseboat in the harbor. It was in the last slip at the end of the pier.

Bill was anxiously waiting her arrival on the top deck of the boat. He looked very excited to see her. "Ahoy there!" Willow smiled vigorously and waved back to acknowledge him as she got out of the car. While walking up the gangplank from the dock to the boat, she caught sight of a large fishtail slapping the water. Willow was mesmerized as she watched it making lazy figure eights in the secluded harbor. Once on board, Bill greeted her with a welcoming smile and a hearty New England handshake. He politely asked about the drive and inquired whether she would like some lunch.

"Yes, I'd love some! It was exhausting and I didn't really have a chance to stop along the way to get a bite to eat."

Offering her a seat, he said. "Ok, make yourself comfortable and I'll fix a couple sandwiches. Be right back!"

She replied, "Thank you, that would be great!" While Willow was getting situated in a comfortable deck chair and finally starting to unwind, relaxing after the long drive, she glimpsed the same fishtail she had seen earlier. It glistened in the afternoon sun. Water droplets were sparkling across the length and breadth of it. The fish appeared to be moving closer and closer to the boat with every swish of its tail. As quickly as it appeared, it disappeared. Just then, Bill emerged from the galley with the food.

"Thank you so much, it looks yummy. I was about ready to collapse from hunger!" she said with anticipation.

Bill responded graciously. "You're very welcome. After lunch, I'll bet you'd like to meet Oceana too...huh?"

Glancing around, Willow enthusiastically replied, "Oh, I would. Is she nearby?"

Bill looked out over the railing. "Well, yes. She's been swimming around the boat for a little while now."

He scanned the water and waited. Then, he caught sight of the young mermaid as she completely emerged. Pointing towards aft, he said, "She's just there."

Willow pushed her chair back and hastily stood up. "I thought that was a dolphin or a really big fish swimming in the harbor!"

Bill chuckled to himself and then replied, "Well, yes, she is part fish and kinda big." Oceana appeared alongside the boat. She had a timid, shy smile on her face. Willow stared, too stunned to speak.

"Come over and meet our guest, Oceana." While keeping her body close to the railing, she stayed carefully concealed so as not to be seen. She rose up to meet Willow, who extended her hand downward to greet her.

"I'm very happy to make your acquaintance at last." Oceana nodded, then smiled, acknowledging she understood. When Oceana came to live with Bill, he devised a method of hand signs and pictures to communicate with her. These were necessary for the development of their relationship. He drew a picture of Willow, standing with others, with the word "Warriors" over the group.

"Oceana, Willow has a group of friends called The Warriors who are fighting to protect and save the Earth. She wants to invite you and Zippy to join them. Do you understand?"

Suddenly, out of nowhere, Zippy appeared and snuggled close to Oceana's ear. They were blissfully in a world of their own, as they lovingly cooed at each other. It was a sight Willow would never forget.

In an encouraging tone, Bill repeated his question. "Do you and Zippy want to be a part of The Warriors?"

Oceana looked up into his kind eyes and nodded yes.

Bill smiled, quickly turning to Willow, "There, you have your answer!"

In a moment of sheer joy, Willow exclaimed, "Fantastic! I can't wait to tell the others! We were wondering how we'd conduct engagements in the water since the oceans are becoming so littered with plastic and other pollutants. With global warming, tropical storms and hurricane activity at an all-time high, we must address the crisis in the oceans. Now, we have an aquatic Warrior and her little friend to help us. I'm so thankful. It's a wonderful blessing!"

Oceana proved to be an invaluable member of The Warriors. She may have been a mermaid, but her activism contributed greatly and was an important part of protecting water environments around the globe. However, her involvement did present a challenge. Because she wasn't able to speak English or any other human language, it was difficult to understand her. Through tail slaps and other non-verbal means, like head and hand gestures, Oceana eventually became more widely understood. She communicated with mammals and other sea life with ease and grace. As an aquatic being, who could only be out of the water for brief periods of time, her active participation in engagements with The Warriors was limited, but essential.

In the following months and at the height of the hurricane season off of the Gulf of Mexico, Oceana had her first successful engagement, during which she fought climate change and Disturber forces. Bill functioned as her liaison. During that action, she proved her worth to the team, solidifying her place in the struggle for the coming months. Her journey as a Warrior was just beginning and it would be a long voyage of discovery for all of them.

Oceana rested comfortably along the edge, watching the incoming throng arriving. Once, it was a vibrant hub teeming with life. It represented the heart of a thriving ecology that burst with color and energy. All that remained was an empty stretch of coastal rock formation. It became pale and washed out and reflected decades of pollution from chemical substances, deposited by humans, which bleached every inch of healthy coral found in the underwater seascape.

Oceana swished her broad tail, treading water, anxiously awaiting the arrival of the schools of fish of all species, as well as dolphins, turtles and other sea life. Today's engagement would serve as a bold attempt at the end of this season to change the currents of the ocean and to divert a potent hurricane, heading for the Southeastern seaboard of Florida and the Texas Panhandle. The goal was to find a way to turn it back out to sea.

Out of the corner of her eye, Oceana caught sight of a familiar figure darting back and forth. She tried to focus her attention on the small creature, but it moved too fast. Before she knew what was happening, it snuggled next to her ear. It was Zippy, the seahorse, who joined Oceana on all her aquatic adventures. He was her constant companion and guardian and always close by when needed. The two friends communicated in a series of loving gurgles and chirps, which resembled buzzing and whirring sounds a hummingbird makes flitting from flower to flower. They exchanged affectionate eye contact and swam around each other as a form of acknowledgement. This was going to be a large engagement and since, Oceana would be occupied conducting the event, she gave Zippy instructions to alert her if there was danger. He served as an alarm system to head off any Disturber forces attempting to upset their plans.

During their tender reunion, vast schools of fish were forming along the reef, spanning a wide margin. There was a huge distance to cover. It encompassed the Gulf of Mexico, which was the backbone of an intricate and delicate ecosystem. Every kind of species was represented, from the smallest angelfish to the largest humpback whale. They combined their flippers, fins and tails to create a massive energetic force so as to churn the waters and redirect the currents away from land and back out to sea. It was a bold action and an intervention geared at diverting the frigid Arctic meltwater from spilling into and mixing with the warmer, southern water. When those two waters combined, an increase in tropical storms and hurricane activity occurred.

After becoming aware of their arrival, Oceana swam to an outcropping of rock, hovering above it and settling on the most prominent point. She spoke to the assembly in a universally recognized language similar to whale-song, which was generally understood by all. In a series of long, lilting moans that changed in pitch, she communicated in a soothing tone that the majority interpreted and responded to without any difficulty. At great length and intricate detail, she explained the task at hand and what was at stake.

It involved a Herculean effort to agitate the ocean through massive fish locomotion. The hope was to bring about the necessary movement through flippers, fins and tales, which, in turn, would stir the waters with enough force so as to redirect the incoming hurricane and stop it from making landfall. The throng positioned themselves directly throughout the current at the most powerful point of convergence, proceeding to work as a unit while the action officially got underway.

Nearby, in an isolated cove, a small motor boat was anchored. Aboard were two henchmen who worked for The Disturbers. They were under orders to attack and destroy Warriors on land and sea. Today, they had their sights set firmly on Oceana even though she was committed to saving the environment and countless species of animal and plant life in the path of the hurricane; her actions could also protect those same Disturber forces who were hellbent on destruction as well. Their orders were clear; they must eliminate her by any means at their disposal. As a Warrior, she was a symbol of change and a threat to their way of life. The Disturbers' mission was to maintain control over the world's economy through various corrupting influences. Dumpster and Trasher were dispatched to the scene to protect those interests and remove any obstacles.

Wearing wetsuits, they swam to the site of the engagement as quietly as possible so as not to be noticed. Trasher was armed with a speargun. Not far away, on cruise control and staying close by to protect Oceana, Zippy spied the two shadowy figures. They bobbed up and down in the water like two empty pop bottles, very noticeable and easy to spot. In an instant, Zippy sped back to Oceana to tell her of their presence. He chirped loudly and nuzzled close to her ear. After acknowledging the threat, she thanked him and quickly returned to directing the myriad forms of aquatic life in the engagement.

Trasher, the smaller of the two henchmen, observed from a reasonable distance. While smirking at Dumpster, he pointed, "Hey, I see her! Wait a minute…say, she's not too bad…kinda cute! Are you sure we're supposed to get rid of her or just scare her away?"

Dumpster barked back, "Don't be a putz, Trash! If you've got a shot, take aim and get rid of her, dude!"

Trasher was mildly confused, which was the state he

was frequently in. He shrugged his shoulders. "Okay, whatever you say." He swam a bit closer in order to get in better position for his shot. While on patrol, Zippy caught sight of Trasher readying the speargun. Suddenly, just as Oceana was conducting the next group out to sea, a sharp projectile whizzed by grazing her side. She whirled around quickly, without batting an eyelash, calling upon a school of Electrophorus electricus, otherwise known as electric eel, to reply to the attack. Zippy made a mad dash to be by her side, so upset by what he witnessed, since he was unable to protect his dearest friend. The eels swarmed over, around and through from every side, completely engulfing their targets in a shower of electrical impulses. They laid down such a barrage of stings, zaps and shocks that they forced the divers to retreat, fleeing at full speed. Swimming as fast as their flippers would go, Trasher yelped and turned to the other, "You know, Dump, the boss ain't gonna like this!"

With the henchman on the run, Zippy stayed close by Oceana's side so she could return to overseeing the engagement. The fish-fueled locomotion was having a massive impact on the flow of the currents, creating the desired effect. The intention of the action was to cause a change in the eco-stasis and reverse an established pattern. The huge schools of fish, along with other mammals, took turns churning the waters in sequence. As one group tired, another would take their place. The group's movements resembled those of a ballet company performing perfect tendus with absolute precision. The group combined seamlessly, working in unison, demonstrating coordination and intricate timing with every move. It was estimated to take approximately eight hours, which was just long enough to hold off the projected arrival of the storm. Only after completion of the task, would they know if the daring adventure was a success The Warriors hoped it would be.

Chapter 5

The Disturbers

"Oh what a tangled web we weave when first we practice to deceive." - Sir Walter Scott

The beginning of the 18th Century marked the arrival of the Industrial Revolution, which drove the economy of developing countries. Grit and opportunism brought progress. The aim was to provide conveniences, viewed as indispensable, for an ever-changing modern society that was clambering for the latest product innovations. These conveniences also filled the consumer niche, which fueled the growing demand for a better quality of life.

The tremendous hunger for the Earth's natural resources brought about wholesale harvesting in countries around the world. During this era, the once plentiful forests suffered major losses. Trees served as the raw material for constructing houses, bridges and other structures; these were the basic building blocks of all urban and rural infrastructure. In those days, safeguards to protect the future of fragile ecological environments and to regulate the logging industry hadn't been implemented. In 1905, the United States Department of Forestry came into existence; its mission was to oversee and preserve public lands.

Forests that took hundreds of years to establish and fully mature couldn't renew fast enough to accommodate human population growth. Rather than considering responsible alternatives that employ sustainable harvesting practices, the logging industry operated insatiably, without regard for the natural world. It was oblivious to the glaring negative impact inflicted on the environment and the soil erosion that permanently scarred the land, and to the loss of animal and avian habitats, both of which have long-lasting effects to the present day.

There were other unsustainable industries, besides logging, that operated elsewhere around the world as well. Oil extraction is one such polluting industry still active today more than ever before. Despite the alarming warning signs, it continues to degrade the environment. Its activities decrease the ozone layer and increase C02 levels, both of which contribute to the global warming crisis. Powerful Disturber forces are driven solely by greed and use these harmful practices to undermine the Earth's well-being. That is why The Oracle, Mother

Earth, appealed to a young person like Willow to get involved. She viewed her as a catalyst for change who could develop a solution to the current existential threat. It was imperative for Mother Earth to reach out and connect with people to stem the tide of total destruction.

The Disturber forces were headquartered in The Big Apple. They were strategically located in Manhattan's financial district, which was at the heart of New York City. This was the last great bastion of capitalism and the undisputed epicenter of the business world. The singular, sinister purpose of these profiteers was to plunder the Earth of its natural resources by any means. Their selfish objectives drove them to make money for themselves and their investors without a second thought or show of concern for the planet's long-term survival. These individuals weren't interested in the places they wreaked havoc on or how their laser-focused actions manipulated governments, economies and environments, all for the sake of money.

Never satisfied, they only wanted more. Their goal was to make money and to increase their bottom line. So, what if making a profit involved clear-cutting a pristine old-growth forest? So, what if drilling to extract fossil fuels deep within the earth expelled noxious CO2 gasses, which, when burned, destroyed the atmosphere in the process? So, what if untreated wastewater poured into and polluted rivers and oceans? So, what if these destructive actions indiscriminately threatened all forms of life? To hell with the needless deaths of so many animal species and the irreversible damage that was caused. Who cared as long as the corporations made a profit! The Disturbers were directly responsible for these and other negative impacts heaped upon the Earth.

At the close of the year, smack dab in the middle of a cold New York City day, a meeting of Disturber forces was getting underway. The clandestine meeting was made up of privileged, older white males. It was to discuss new, diabolical ways to thwart the efforts of Willow's Warriors to protect the environment. The Disturbers mandate was clear; to prevent The Warriors from carrying out their higher purpose of saving the planet.

The leader was GD, short for The Great Disturber, the Chairman of the Board. He was a cruel, egotistical man and a pompous old windbag who headed up the villainous organization. Just beneath him in the pecking order was Disturber 1, the CEO of Forensic Motors. They were the creators of the gas-guzzling fossil fuel vehicles, the Triceratops 4000, the T-Rex 5000, and the latest monstrosity, the Mastodon 9000 UAV (Urban Assault Vehicle). Next, was Disturber 2, the CEO of the Frick and Frack Oil corporation, which was strategically located in the Texas Panhandle. These individuals were the captains of the industry. They were the spawn of a long line of environmental exploiters who degraded and threatened the earth and the existence of every living being on the planet.

Dumpster and Trasher, two of the Disturber henchmen, were also in attendance. Dumpster and Trasher were code names for their diabolical natures and for the unpleasant, dirty deeds they carried out. The Disturbers used them like lackeys on assignments to stop The Warriors. Lastly, the organization's attorney, Lucien Higgenbotham, was a mastermind at the art of deception and not to be overlooked or undone. He was a corrupt, sinister individual, who represented them in their exploitative and nefarious activities around the world.

The blast of a woman's voice broke through the din of generalized chatter while managing to rise above the excessive noise level in the boardroom. "Order! Come to order, gentleman!" The Disturbers secretary and assistant to the Chairman, Ms. Mathilda Bottleneck, made this shrill sound as she attempted to convene the board meeting. She was a petite, older woman with old-fashioned, horn-rimmed glasses. Her powerful voice was much larger than her actual size. She bellowed loudly, so that she could be heard across the huge boardroom without any difficulty. The irritating voice roused the full body of the assemblage; it also raised hairs on the back of each and every neck while sending shivers down the spines of those in attendance. She was in the unique position of being the only woman in the room at the day's proceedings. At first glance, and to the casual observer, those congregating there looked more like a rogue's gallery of the criminal element rather than members of the executive set.

After a call to order, Trasher was the first speaker to

be recognized. "Boss, I just wanna say I had nothing to do with that mermaid thing. My speargun jammed… it misfired by accident. That blond fish girl was lucky--she was so damn quick that day. Ya, but hey, boss, why are we tryin' to get rid of her anyway? I think she's kinda cute...heh, heh, heh, if you know what I mean…"

Trasher winked one eye slyly while smirking at GD. Dumpster wore a frown and looked his usual disgusted self, while shooting a hostile, sideways glance in Trasher's direction, "Pipe down, you nincompoop!"

He quickly swung around in his chair and pleaded the case to GD, "Hey, boss, I'm not responsible for *his* mistakes...if he'd aimed straight instead of trying to check out her flashy, swishin' tail, we'd all have one less Warrior to worry about!"

Before the other henchman could retort, GD silenced them both with a dismissive wave of his hand accompanied by an angry scowl. Raising his voice, he pointed a gnarled finger in their faces. "You incompetent fools can't be trusted to carry out even the simplest of assignments! You fail me constantly at every turn! This is just the latest in a long line of blunders and muck-ups! It may be your last! However, since I'm feeling generous today, you may get a second chance to redeem yourselves."

He cocked his head to one side and looked directly at Lucien as he spoke, "What do we hear from our partners in crime down in that Brazilian hell hole?"

Lucien was a devious man who resembled a gargoyle. He had sharp, pointy, menacing features. There was a wicked-sounding bent to his voice. He replied deliberately, "All is going well, as we expected. They're playing right into our hands, GD. The government is cooperating with us by having their people set fire to the forest to clear the land so that we can use it for whatever we want." He appeared self-satisfied as he spoke. A cynical grin was permanently plastered on his face.

GD replied, "Well, just last week, I had a perfect phone call with El Presidente, who assured me we would have no problems moving forward with our current plans to build luxury townhomes and a golf course on the site."

The CEO of Frick and Frack Oil Disturber 1 interrupted, chiming in, "One problem, boss, is that do-gooder activist, Capricio di Leonardis. He's stirring up the natives and donating money to help fight the fires. Sticking up for their friggin' indigenous rights."

Then Disturber 2 added, "Yeah, and that's not all. I heard Willow's Warriors might get involved too. Sheesh... where'd they get such a stupid name?"

GD, who was deep in thought, stared blankly into space. He paused for a moment and then turned toward Dumpster and Trasher, casting a steely gaze. "Now, you two will get the chance you've been waiting for. I'll send you down there, and this time I don't want any mistakes, or heads will roll!" The two twitchy henchmen eagerly nodded in obedient compliance. With one immobilizing glance, he telegraphed fear that pierced them to the bone.

They were frozen to their chairs. Dumpster spoke first, "Well, ah...well...what do you want us to do, boss?"

Trasher, unable to restrain himself, blurted out, "Should I bring my speargun too? Huh? He looked around the room for reassurance. I promise I won't miss! I'll get em' this time, boss!"

"Silence, you fools! We'll set a trap for them. That busybody, Capricio, and those Warriors won't see it coming or be able to wriggle out of it. Finally, we'll be rid of them for good! Once and for all!" GD said imperiously, puffing out his chest as he spoke. He turned again to his attorney, "Lucien, how quickly can we get the Pterodactyl 1 gassed up and ready to fly?"

"Well, it's ready to go now GD--standing by at JFK as we speak."

"Great! Ok, pack your bags, boys. You're taking a trip down south and I don't mean Florida." He laughed as he spoke, with a twisted smirk on his sour puss. Both henchmen looked wide-eyed and bewildered. They quickly stood up and snapped to attention, both bumping into one another while alternately tripping over everything in sight. He shook his head in pure disgust as he received similar reactions and a general consensus of opinion from D1 and D2.

GD added, "It's no wonder Willow and her Warriors keep getting the best of us. Look what we've got to work with! A couple of botched fools and bungled dimwits!" NOW, I'm running the show! Let's see just how far this bunch of so-called 'crusaders' get with their plans! Those busybodies are like a wad of gum stuck on the bottom of my shoe that is impossible to get off!"

GD was proud of his ability to analyze any complicated situation. He composed himself and proceeded to address the board members, "Okay, all you high-priced windbags, what ideas can you come up with to combat Willow's Warriors once we get down there? Come on now, what am I paying you for anyway?"

D2 spoke up first rather reluctantly. He suggested they run them over with one of his gas-guzzling vehicles. The latest monstrosity from Forensic Motors was the huge Mastodon 9000 UAV (Urban Assault Vehicle), fully equipped and capable of mowing down anything in its path. That particular idea wasn't very well received by the boss, who was now sporting a permanent scowl during the meeting.

The next deep thinker brave enough to speak up was D1. He suggested, "I know, let's trick 'em into going into the forest like they're trying to save it or something and when they get in far enough…light it on fire!"

Showing equal disdain for that idea as well, GD shook his head. "Ok, Lucien, you're up. What have you got for me? It better be good, buddy."

Looking devilishly wicked as he casually leaned back in his swivel chair, smiling in his usual devious way, he said, "Why use force against them? If we get our people in the government on the payroll to help us out, we can slap an injunction on them. We could stop their actions on the grounds that they're interfering in a foreign country's affairs. Better yet, we might find a way to blame the whole sordid affair on that meddling activist, Capricio di Leonardis!"

GD smiled from ear to ear and nodded to acknowledge his approval while breaking into spontaneous, boisterous laughter, "Aha, very good! Now you're talking!

Capital idea Lucien! That's the best suggestion I've heard so far...we'll beat em' at their own game, fair and square, without lifting a finger to do it!"

"Yes, GD," Lucien smirked, "It will be good for our capital, too!" They both guffawed heartily at the humor while slapping each other on the back.

GD inquired, "What will it take to get our Brazilian friends on board with our development plans going forward? What kind of payoffs are they demanding for their services?"

Lucien replied in his uniquely dry, detached way, "Well, GD, we've got the newly elected president on our side down there. What's more, he wants a piece of our action, and he wants it pretty damn bad!"

GD calmly asked, "Oh, yeah...really? What does he want, Lucien?"

"Well, he's an ambitious, greedy sort, that one. After the thugs and mercenaries he hired laid waste to their own country by starting those fires, all he asked for in return was"...Lucien paused, sporting a devilish grin. The members of the organization propped themselves up straight in their high back chairs, providing their full attention. They hung on Lucien's every word.

"Okay, spit it out! What's he want?" GD barked.

"Just for us to make him President for life! What do you think about that, huh?" The sensational revelation was followed by a cacophony of laughs, snorts, and snickers that echoed around the room. Choice comments were heard. "Who does he think he is anyway?" and "We could have easily done the job by ourselves without the rest of them getting in our way!"

GD shouted at the top of his lungs, "Silence, you dimwitted fools!" That's absolutely correct, Lucien. We must have those two-bit politicians in our pockets to get control of their resources. Without their cooperation, it would be all but impossible to have our way in those third-world sinkholes. It's good for our business and it's plenty good for them too. Lucien, I want you to draw up a document stating that the despot be made President for life. As usual, once we get what we want down there, you'll get rid of him, kick him out of office right away?"

Lucien acknowledged the request with a nod of his head as he hungrily licked his lips. He enjoyed this part of his job the most. Dutifully, he punctuated the command with his standard response, "Consider it done, boss!"

"Now for the last order of business," GD bellowed. "Another one of Willow's Warriors, a member of the Anti-Fractivists, named Rowdy, is down at one of F&F's oil refineries at our Texas Panhandle operation. He and some others are causing trouble; they're all part of that ragtag group of teenage misfits. They're sabotaging our operations by staging public protests and claiming we're causing too much air pollution." The boardroom was a whirl of raucous, nervous energy which was punctuated by a collective moan, a shaking of heads and pounding of fists.

GD continued, "We have a recent clip of him from a

public forum of the Railroad Commission during this past week." GD turned to Ms. Bottleneck signaling her to run the footage. Rowdy appeared on the screen. He was making an address to the Railroad Commission, the governing body of the oil and gas industry in Texas. He stood up proudly, speaking in a clear, persuasive voice. "My words are for you people who sit in authority over us. Your sanctimonious right-wing drivel that supports your selfish interests while claiming loyalty to our planet is selling our birthright for the love of money and power. You're not our elders or leaders, and, therefore, we're not bound by your rules or obliged to obey your laws. We will not back down and we'll stand together as long as it takes until assurances are given by the Frick and Frack Oil Co., that they will reduce polluting emissions at their Texas oil refining facility! We have rights as human beings that cannot be trampled on or taken away and we will stand up for them!"

"That's enough!" GD roared. "We've had that stupid Commission in our back pocket for years now. Why can't they block the actions of those troublemakers?"

Directing his next question to Lucien, "I want that punk, Rowdy, and the rest of his band of merry men arrested! Can you handle it?"

Lucien sported a patented sly grin on his face. He calmly replied, "Yes, GD, consider it done."

"Then what are you waiting for? Let's get this show on the road!" GD bellowed. The assembled body exploded in a whirl of disoriented, frenetic energy. Like cockroaches scattering to hide when a light is turned on.

He jeered as he spoke, "That's right, leave you

incompetent fools!" He looked in the direction of his assistant. He was stern and steely-eyed, which gave her all the visual instruction she needed to end the meeting with just one look.

Matilda swung the gavel firmly while simultaneously screeching, "This meeting is adjourned!"

Part One

The Journey into the Sacred Forest

Chapter 6

Em Chamas no Brasil (Up in Flames in Brazil)

"The clearest way into the universe is through a forest wilderness." - John Muir

The fires burned out of control as they swept through the Amazon Rainforest of Brazil. At the first of the year, Juniper and Sequoia, bonafide members of Willow's Warriors, headed south to lend a hand. The Tree Huggers, as they were called, devoted themselves to protecting forests. In this particular engagement, the objective was to stop the fires from raging out of control while preventing Disturber Forces from receiving favors from a corrupt Brazilian government. DF's had been stirring up trouble by mucking up the system, both politically and environmentally, for quite a while. They were directly responsible for contributing to the demise of the country's most precious resource, known as "the lungs of the earth."

Since they hailed from Tillamook County, Oregon, the Tree Huggers were very familiar with the destruction of forested lands. Both were raised in the oxygen-rich climate of the Pacific Northwest, which served as the perfect backdrop for their upbringing and education as activists. It instilled in them a deep appreciation of the land. As young girls, they witnessed many bitter battles over clear-cutting between logging interests and environmental protestors. Family members were torn between their loyalties to the company, which were in direct conflict with their love of the land. The economy of the community was precariously intertwined with the lumber industry. Locals were dependent, but also provided preservation and protection to the sacred woodlands.

The relationship with the industry was an unhealthy alliance. Since logging was the means to make a living in the area, it operated as a control mechanism over the resident's well-being. It generated revenue, provided economic stability and everyone relied on it as a means of survival in some way, shape or form.

Young people there grew up like Willow. They lived in multi-generational families that were tethered to the earth. In much the same way, they spent their otherwise idyllic childhoods exploring and experiencing the wonders of creation, though influenced by upheaval and tensions too. The battleground was where the lines of conflict were philosophically drawn around the value of trees in the worldwide marketplace. They were viewed strictly as a significant monetary commodity.

Sequoia and Juniper were raised in the city of Coos

Bay near the Elliott State Forest. It was where the last track of old growth Redwoods in Tillamook County, Oregon, was located. When such forests were plentiful, logging, specifically clearcutting, was a common practice. After decades of insatiable cutting with no plan for renewal, 82,000 acres of public land, now under the protection of the Bureau of Land Management, remained.

The demand for building materials and paper products of all kinds was the impetus that moved local economies forward, but the demand also posed a threat to the long-term health of the fragile ecosystem. Meeting the enormous pressure of human population growth has always burdened natural resources. Trees, in particular, serve a higher purpose. Through photosynthesis, they expel oxygen which then absorbs harmful carbon emissions that accumulate in the atmosphere. Trees also provide diverse animal and avian species a habitat, which contributes to the survival of the planet.

The Tree Huggers, sunk deep in an environmental context, formed a strong bond to the earth as they were aligned with the belief that nature is sacred. They made a pact to become involved and wholeheartedly devoted to the cause. Drawn to the intriguing message Willow posted on social media, Sequoia and Juniper responded with great enthusiasm as their shared experiences had a common thread. Their backgrounds were similar to Willow's and they felt as though they might have found a niche; encountering difficulties and conflicts in their struggle to protect the planet, which were all too familiar.

Willow was deeply impressed by how well the girls were to be Warriors. After their initial discussion, she invited them to join the group. As they were also in the last year of high school, Willow suggested they take a sabbatical to do a senior project as she had done and complete it in the field. This would be an excellent way to follow their dreams and learn how to become environmental activists. As they were underaged, they had to receive parental consent as well. Teacher involvement was also mandatory. While away, they had to be supervised weekly online.

When the fires swept through the Amazon, their collaborative efforts proved to be useful. Willow decided to send the girls to link up with Italian actor and "boots on the ground" environmentalist Capricio di Leonardis. He and his foundation were providing resources, financial aid and advocacy to the indigenous people of the Brazilian rainforest since the outbreak of the fires. Willow reasoned that the Tree Huggers' previous experience in the Pacific Northwest made them the best choice to send on the assignment.

Willow reached out to billionaire/philanthropist and The Warriors' benefactor, Sam Teyer, to finance the trip. He was ethically, morally and philosophically committed to the cause and aided them completely in all their activities. He was one of the few super-wealthy, one percent, that actually cared about protecting the Earth. He provided the necessary support and funds that gave them the freedom to operate and do this important work around the world.

After travel arrangements to Brazil were made, the girls got underway. The plan was to contact Capricio when they arrived at the Antonio Carlos Jobim International Airport in Rio de Janeiro. He would be their guide and mentor. Teaching them what they needed to know and how to get started on the assignment.

After the long flight and as the plane descended toward the runway, both girls were barely able to contain their excitement. They eagerly anticipated what lay ahead.

"I wonder if Capricio will have his cell phone on him when we call?" Juniper asked nervously.

"J, of course he will. What do you think, huh? He's a famous, sophisticated movie star, not some goofy flake," Sequoia replied.

"How do you know, S. I mean, aren't most guys you know... kinda weird and strange?"

Sequoia shook her head in disbelief. "Girl, I've got to get you out more!"

Juniper chuckled, "Hey S, I heard Rio's got a heck of a nightlife. We should check out what's happening while we're here."

"Sounds like fun, I know... but we're both too young to get into clubs and besides, we're here to do a job. Don't forget… Willow's depending on us!"

"Oh, what a drag! I was really looking forward to that. Brazilian guys are supposed to be muy caliente!" She winked playfully. "Yeah and wow, that accent is so sexy! It gets me every time!"

"It will be a miracle if we find time to eat, let alone

go out dancing and meet cute guys… come on, J. Stay focused!" Sequoia said, halfway giving herself the pep talk too, as she spoke. Juniper smiled to herself, nodding shyly, reluctantly agreeing with her friend.

When the plane touched down, the roar of the engines made a deafening sound as the brakes were applied. When it pulled into the terminal, the girls peered out the window to look for anyone fitting Capricio's description.

"I don't see him, S," Juniper sighed heavily.

"Give him some time. He might be hiding or something to avoid alerting Disturber forces to his presence," she said with confidence. "Hurry, J! Get your things and let's go meet him!"

They deplaned and headed for the gate, actively scanning the area for any sign of Capricio. While they were busy looking around, a man casually strolled toward them. He looked to be a native tribesman in his early forties. He was dressed in traditional clothing, wearing a simple tunic and loincloth. His black hair hung straight down to his shoulders. It was loosely held together by a colorful bandana which was tied around his head. Standing nearby, but slightly behind him, was a young, curvaceous woman of about twenty.

Sequoia whispered confidently, "She must be his daughter."

While pointing to the young woman, he said, "Hello, my name is Orfeo...and this is my wife, Mira." The girls stared blankly at each other. They tried not to show their surprise and didn't say a word.

Addressing the man politely, Sequoia spoke first. “Hello, this is Juniper and my name is Sequoia. We're The Tree Huggers”. Orfeo acknowledged her greeting with a cordial nod of his head. “A friend of ours, Capricio di Leonardis, was supposed to meet us here... do you know him?”

“Yes, I do. He sent me here. I'm sorry, but he won't be coming. The Polícia Federal are holding him for questioning about the fires, replied Orfeo.

Juniper blurted out, “What do you mean? They think HE started them?”

“He's well known, so they blame this on him,” continued Orfeo. ‘We know they aren't telling the truth to cover up their actions.”

“I went to see him this morning, and he asked me to pick you up from the airport and take you to a place of safety. If you're ready, let's get going.” Orfeo and Mira ushered the girls into a Chevy Opala Caravan and drove them back to the city.

On the way, Sequoia nudged Juniper with her elbow. “Let's call Willow tonight and give her the lowdown on what's goin' on here, ok?”

She agreed, “Sounds like a plan, S.”

After getting settled in, Sequoia called Willow. She explained Capricio's situation and asked for advice about how to proceed.

“Willow, I've got some bad news about Capricio. We've been told he's being held. No, they haven't arrested him yet. It seems they're only holding him to get him out of the way for now." Her tone was noticeably strained and edgy as she spoke.

Willow replied calmly, "I think it's time to get Peter involved with his legal expertise." She referred to Peter Kensington, The Warrior's attorney, who represented them in these matters. He was always available when needed and provided his services pro bono, viewing environmental protection as the highest priority.

"Peter is still down in Texas mopping up after the last Anti-Frack engagement. The guys got arrested after exercising their civil rights, protesting the air pollution problems at the Frick and Frack Oil refinery. It's an ongoing struggle. Rowdy has been gone so long now I wonder if I'll ever see him again. As soon as possible, I'll send Peter down your way, hopefully in the next couple of days, to get to the bottom of these trumped-up charges. You know, Sequoia...this situation has Disturber written all over it!"

"You're right. We'll keep an eye out for him here." Happy with Willow's response, she breathed a huge sigh of relief to hear that help was on its way.

"You guys just hang in there and focus on getting that business wrapped up as soon as possible. If everything goes well, we'll have you back home before the end of the week, ok?"

"Yes, we will! Thanks, Willow, you're a lifesaver!"

Early the next morning, Sequoia and Juniper awoke to the sound of macaws squawking and fluttering about, filling the courtyard with sound. It was something neither one had ever experienced before. Quite an alarm clock for the two naive travelers! Once dressed, they went downstairs to a simple breakfast of finger bananas, pineapple juice, pão francês (french bread) and a delightful Brazilian coffee.

Juniper, in her usual brash way, didn't hesitate to ask, "What's been happening down here, Orfeo? Who's stirring up all this trouble?" By this time, it was apparent to the girls that Orfeo was the tribal elder of his people in all matters relating to the sacred rainforest where he and the Yanomami lived.

"We've been watching the government and strange men from the outside come into our home for a while now. They take more and more every time they come. They're pushing us deeper into the forest because they want our land. Now, they return again, these men from the outside, to make us go."

Juniper turned to Sequoia, speaking very frankly, "S, those other men, they sound a lot like Disturbers to me."

Sequoia thought for a moment. "Yes, J. I think you're right," Sequoia addressed Orfeo, "We've got a plan to get Capricio away from the Federais and back here safely. In a couple of days, our attorney, Peter Kensington, will be coming from the United States to argue for his release. We will try to put legal pressure on the government until they let him go. In the meantime... what are you doing about the fires?"

"The people are working to stop the outsiders from starting new fires. As soon as we put them out the next day they start again. We would give our lives to protect our home, but we don't know what else we can do.

Capricio helped us in many ways, with money and food, before they captured him. The government says he started the fires, so they can point the finger of blame on him! They're doing this so we won't know the truth, but we see everything. The government is destroying the forest to grow soybeans, raise cattle, and put up their buildings. They don't care about anything else, except money!"

The girls decided to stay out of sight and lay low until Peter arrived from the States. It wouldn't do any good for them to be noticed. They didn't have long to wait. Willow came through as promised, and on their third day in Rio, Peter arrived. Both were surprised at just how quickly he came. The girls and Orfeo met him at the airport. He was an older man in his early 70's and was attired in casual, tropical wear. His long wavy hair was steel gray in color, and he wore it back in a ponytail. He was a seasoned activist and part of the counterculture revolution of the turbulent sixties. He marched in protest over the Vietnam War and during a time when questioning authority was one's patriotic duty. Peter earned his reputation defending radicals who were committed to social change and his professional services were always in high demand.

Striding confidently toward the waiting party, Peter formally introduced himself, "You two must be The Tree Huggers. Willow told me all about you." He bowed slightly at the waist, "I'm Peter Kensington, Esq. at your service."

Sequoia smiled graciously while gesturing toward

their host. "Peter, this is Orfeo of the Yanomami tribe. He will take us to the place where they're holding Capricio."

Like a true gentleman, Peter politely acknowledged the greeting. He extended his hand to Orfeo. "Very nice to meet you all. Now, if you don't mind, let's get acquainted on the way, shall we?"

The group set out on the walk toward the Delegacia de Polícia. It was the place where Capricio was being held. Orfeo told Peter that he attempted to tell the authorities that Capricio was his guest the whole time while he was in Brazil and it was impossible for him to have started the fires. Since the first of the year, he'd tried explaining that fact to them. They refused to listen to his story and chose to ignore it completely.

Orfeo was the leader of his people. He was held in high esteem, revered, and honored as a shaman. The non-native population treated him like a savage and showed no regard for his status. Orfeo and Capricio were working on strategies to stop the mercenaries who operated without restraint and frightened the native tribes out of their sacred forest home by threatening the people and their families on a daily basis. Once Capricio was out of the way, they resumed their activities, setting fires to destroy the forest and clear the land.

The long, narrow path to the station was crooked. It wound around and rose in elevation. The girls were in great physical shape and took the hilly two-mile walk with ease. Their destination lay on the outskirts of Rio in Galeão. As the party was nearing the station, they saw off in the distance, a sinister cast of characters forming together just outside the building. The whole bunch looked desperate and cutthroat. At first glance, one would think them capable of doing any kind of dastardly deed for an American dollar or Brazilian real. Peter cautioned the girls not to look at them directly or listen to anything they might say. He told them to focus their sights on the path and stay on track. The group was intent on its purpose, moving forward and drawing closer with every step. The thugs stood firm barricading themselves in the entrance to the station. Peter and Orfeo formed a shield in front of the girls to protect them. Just before a fracas broke out, the doors swung wide open. An official-looking man stepped out, dressed in military garb.

"My name is Captain Tomaso... state your business here!" Peter introduced himself and the others, then inquired about their friend. He asked why they were holding him. The Captain looked stern and wooden as he replied that Capricio was there. The official response was "for his own safety." With all the decorum and diplomacy Peter could muster, he requested to see Capricio. The Captain gave consent. Turning quickly on his heels, he motioned for Peter to follow him as they went in the general direction of the detention area. After walking through a narrow passageway to one of the holding areas at the back of the building, they came to a cell mostly in shadow. It was a dark, dreary and very inhospitable place. Peter called out loudly, "Capricio, are you in there?"

A man's voice replied back through the empty void, "Yes, I'm here." The Captain opened the door and ushered Peter in. An exasperated gasp could be heard upon seeing a friendly face. Peter calmly reassured Capricio with a pat on the back he'd come to help.

"My friend, can you tell me about the events leading up to your detainment? What are you being questioned about?" Peter inquired.

"They accused me of starting the rainforest fires and interfering in the affairs of the Brazilian government. I've been staying with the Yanomami, never out of their sight the whole time while I've been in Brazil!" He glared at the Captain as he spoke.

"The charge is completely bogus; nothing to worry about. I have a writ that grants you immunity from prosecution as an Italian citizen. They've no proof, evidence, or legal grounds to hold you for any sort of crime. Maybe, not wasting money on partying, like other famous celebrities who come to Brazil, rather helping the indigenous people protect their sacred forest, was just too much for the government to accept." Peter demanded that Capricio be set free at once. He faced toward the cell door and gave Captain Tomaso the document.

After reading the paper, the Captain carefully chose his words, "Look, I don't want any trouble here…just following Mr. Higgenbotham's orders."

Peter frowned as he leaned forward, "Lucien Higgenbotham?"

"Yes." the Captain replied.

"Aha! Now, I see what's been going on here!" His

face turned a brilliant red. ‘Disturber forces have been in this area and they’re responsible for the fires. To cover up their destructive acts, they tried to pin their crimes on Capricio! They will stop at nothing to promote their twisted agenda!” he said forcefully. “Come on, my friend... let’s get you outta here without delay!”

The girls sat inside while Orfeo stayed on guard outside. Sequoia and Juniper looked uneasy, nervously fidgeted while waiting. They were downright scared in these surroundings, but put on a brave face. As Peter emerged from the passageway, he was accompanied by a man the girls recognized from his many film roles as the famous actor Capricio di Leonardis. Greeting them graciously, he said, “Ah, buongiorno ,senoritas.” Smiling at each other while looking at him, they broke into an uncontrollable case of girlish giggles.

Eager to leave and retreat to a place of safety, the group hastened their departure. They traversed the twisted path at a fast pace. As they rounded a bend, the thugs stood waiting in ambush. At the head of the pack was a person quite well-known to Peter. It was the ominous presence of The Disturber’s attorney, Lucien Higgenbotham. He spoke in a haughty, arrogant tone of voice. “WHERE do you think you’re going with this prisoner?”

“Capricio is a free man! You can’t detain him illegally without any proof of a crime!” Peter exclaimed.

Capricio spoke up in a weakened voice that was barely audible, “They want to keep me under wraps, because once I tell the media what I know, the truth will come out about who is really responsible for the fires."

Sequoia and Juniper chimed in without hesitation, "Yeah! Then you guys won't have a leg to stand on!"

Lucien's eyes narrowed to a slit and his mouth curled into a sneer. "Oh, we'll see about that!" He ordered the waiting men to close ranks. They proceeded to surround the party from all sides in order to prevent them from escaping. Before anyone knew what was happening, a hail of blow darts flew through the air from the tree line above, hitting their intended targets. It was as if they were guided by the Universe. The darts were like heat-seeking missiles laser-focused on the marauders and Lucien. The attackers scattered in all directions looking like walking pincushions. Orfeo had instructed the Yanomami tribesmen to be ready and waiting along the path so they could respond to a possible attack from Disturber forces on the return. They limped and moaned as they fled after receiving the pointed message.

"We put the tip of our darts in the liquid of the Ayahuasca vine. It gives people visions and calms the mind while making them more peaceful. They learn a lesson about how to live in harmony with everyone in the forest." Orfeo explained. The darts were an ideal deterrent to respond with a minimum of damage. The Warriors always adhered to this practice when confronting Disturber forces. The girls, Capricio and Peter laughed heartily while celebrating and giving each other high fives.

Lucien returned to the Polícia Federal station. He

stumbled inside, disoriented from the drug-laced dart. He sat down unsteadily, groping for his mobile phone to make a call. “GD, those punks got away! What? I don’t know how! They caught us by surprise. I think it’s time we got those two dimwits, Dumpster and Trasher, back out there setting fires. I recommend we start harassing the natives like before. That’s my advice, alright? Now, if you don’t mind, I really need a nap. They hit us with something, like a poison dart... I think, not sure what it was. Gotta go, I’ll call back later.” Shortly after the call ended, Lucien slumped over and passed out on a cot in one of the cells. Very drowsy, he fell into a deep, dream-laden stupor. His lips slightly parted as he dozed off, drool running out the corners of his mouth.

After returning to the house in Rio, the group made plans to head into the forest to check on the fires. Their number one job was to prevent any new ones from starting and put out those still burning.

Capricio told the group, “When the fires are lit, we send our tribesmen into the places that are most affected. It’s still unknown who is behind them. Our goal is to be in those specific areas when we get word of activity. Also, we’ve seen tire tracks, just on the fringe of the Amazonia border. They appear to be from a huge vehicle of some kind. So far, we haven’t been able to find out what it is. But it’s just a matter of time before we do.”

Sequoia listened intently. She surmised what might be making the tracks, “The Warriors are aware that Forensic Motors, a company run by The Disturbers, has a huge gas-guzzling RV. It’s the latest in a line of unsustainable vehicles they produce. It's called the Mastodon 9000 Urban Assault Vehicle (UAV). Most likely, that's what's making those tracks."

"Hmmm, very interesting. Well, that seems like a strong possibility," he mused. "We'll never know unless we get out there and find one to prove it exists. I've booked us on the next flight leaving tomorrow morning for Manaus. Orfeo and his tribesman will join us there in 3 days. They're traveling overland by foot."

Peter added, "Well, since my work here is done, I've got a plane to catch to the US. I'll let Willow know what's going on here and assure her that all of you are safe. I must say, it was a pleasure meeting everyone. We'll have to do it again sometime under better circumstances, ok?"

Juniper gave him a big hug, as she thanked him. "Yeah, and we're gonna keep it that way, Peter! Obrigado, meu amigo." The girls and Capricio said their goodbyes, waving a fond farewell as he took a taxi to the airport.

Part Two

The Journey into the Sacred Forest

Chapter 7

Amazonia

"The forest is not a collection of entities... it is a place entirely made from strands of relationships." - George Haskell

Early that next morning, the team returned to the Antonio Carlos Jobim International Airport. The Tree Huggers and Capricio boarded a flight for Manaus.

Juniper sighed heavily, "Darn! We didn't even get to go dancing while we were here or meet any cute guys, S!"

Sequoia looked at her with concern. "What is Capricio… huh?"

Juniper grinned, "No, you know what I mean…guys our age."

"Get your head out of the clouds, J! This journey is just the beginning for us and it's not gonna get any easier, so quit thinking about dancing with guys! That's not why we are down here!" Juniper cast her eyes away as she sheepishly agreed. After the flight got underway, they dozed off, lulled by the soothing vibration of the engines into a much-needed sleep. The trip took a little over four hours. They had plenty of time to rest and recuperate from their first adventure and prepare for the next. As the plane was descending into Manaus, Capricio gently awakened the girls with a light tap on the shoulder. "We're here." They roused slowly, yawned and stretched as they began to sit upright in their seats. Capricio pointed out the window at the view, which drew their attention to the vast rainforest spreading out for miles below.

What they saw simply stunned and amazed them. "I can't believe it, S!" Juniper exclaimed. 'I've never seen anything like that before! It seems to go on forever!"

"You'll get used to it, but never get over it. It's pretty inspiring the first time you see the sight of the emerald forest," Capricio remarked. "Once we get to Manaus, one of Orfeo's tribesmen will bring us to their village. There we will eat, rest and make plans for the journey. Tomorrow we'll go into the forest and look for the proof we need to charge The Disturbers with the fires." The girls nodded their approval most heartily.

After arriving, they gathered up their gear and proceeded to deplane with the rest of the passengers. As promised, a member of the Yanomami tribe was waiting at the terminal of the Manaus International Airport. One of Orfeo's men was there to greet the trio. He was smiling and visibly happy to see Capricio.

"Ah, Benito, dia bom!"

"Muito bem, Senhor Capricio, estou feliz em vê-lo. Vamos lá!" Benito gestured for the threesome to follow him as he led them to an old, well-worn Jeep, that was rugged and outfitted for traveling along the rough jungle roads. This was to be their transportation for the 150-mile trek to their intended destination. The ride was through uneven, mountainous terrain, but the girls didn't mind or complain. Neither were afraid of a little hardship. They bounced happily along the whole way and braced themselves, gripping tightly with every ounce of strength they could muster.

While on the road, Capricio inquired as to what the current situation was with the fires.

"Not so good, Senhor. The fires continue to burn wild. Since those men are paid to do this, they won't stop for nothing. We see the tracks from the grande veículo coming from the outside, because nobody knows where it comes from or who's driving. We can't stop them."

Capricio speculated, "The girls think it's some sort of giant RV."

Juniper leaned forward and interjected, "Yeah, it's called a Mastodon 9000."

Two hours later, the Jeep pulled into the encampment. It was a great relief to arrive safely and a pleasure to get their feet back on solid ground. The village was simple and remote. All the hustle and bustle of the city they'd left behind was nowhere to be found. The girls breathed in the rich jungle air, which was heady. It gave them a feeling of euphoria. It was high altitude and truly indescribable. The atmosphere was so clean and pure.

Capricio rested his hand lightly on Sequoia's shoulder and smiled broadly. "See, I told you…it's awe-inspiring, huh? I knew you guys would love it here...that's why it's so important to protect this place."

"Yes, we see that now." Sequoia and Juniper said in unison.

Benito had prepared two huts for their guests' arrival. The accommodations were modest, but more than adequate for their needs. The floors were swept smooth, clean and there were woven grass mats to sleep on.

After settling in, they were invited to join the large communal dinner with the people from the village. The women were gathered around a large pit. They were stirring cooking pots. They prepared peixe nobre (noble fish), roasted plantains and sweet potatoes over the open fire. In addition to this fare, pats of wild honey and a dab of slimy, iridescent matter that neither of the girls could identify rounded out the meal.

Juniper, trying not to look too surprised, blurted out, "That's not a deadly nightshade, is it?"

"No, J., it's not eggplant. I don't know what it is, really." Juniper dipped her fingers into the goo. She swiped across the leaf and placed them in her mouth swallowing hard. An oddly pleasant look appeared on her face, "Hey, this stuff ain't too bad!" Sequoia followed suit immediately, sporting a similar expression after experiencing the unique taste.

Sitting close to the girls, Benito whispered in Juniper's ear, "Termites. We have muitos insetos here, so we eat them every day... muito bom, né?"

"Yeah, real good. I never thought I would ever like the taste of bugs... but I do!" Juniper roared.

They all had a hearty laugh while thoroughly enjoying the rest of the dinner. Capricio explained to the girls, "In the morning, Benito will guide us to where the most recent set of tire tracks were found. From there, we will cover the area and hopefully locate it." Sequoia and Juniper agreed, both nodding their heads at the same time. "Now, we must all get a good night's sleep, as there is lots of work to do tomorrow."

The girls woke at dawn, ready for the long day's journey into the jungle. Attired in hiking boots, loose-fitting shirts and khaki pants, they were raring to go, looking forward to the adventure. Capricio, along with Benito, joined them at the pit. The plan was simple: get to the place where the tracks were last seen, then do a bit of snooping around to see where they lead. Their destination, however, was some ten miles away and would be an arduous hike over difficult ground.

While walking along a steep portion of the trail, Juniper mused, "I've heard this forest is a magical place, S."

Sequoia took her time replying, as she was too awestruck by the surroundings to offer any kind of a response right away. "Yes, I've never seen anything like it and I don't think I ever will. It's simply too fantastic for words." The jungle that laid out before them was an exotic place, filled with many varieties of orchids, brightly colored frogs and long-tailed macaws, to mention a few. It was a visual feast and nothing they had ever experienced could compare to the diversity found there.

Benito looked back at the girls, "Our people are a part of the forest. We live and breathe life from this place... it's our home. We have much sadness for what is happening, a Floresta Esmeralda está morrendo and there is nothing we can do to stop it." The expression on Benito's face was painfully evident to the others as he spoke.

Capricio gently grasped Benito's shoulder and squeezed it in a reassuring way. "That's why I've been here from the beginning since the fires started. We're doing what is needed to stop the destruction and help the people. Nothing is more important than saving the forest."

After an exhausting two-and-a-half-hour hike, the group finally arrived. The place they were now was eerily dead and lifeless. The lush forest behind them fell away and what lay before them was complete desolation. The endless swath of green became an equally endless expanse of wasteland. It was a stark apocalyptic landscape devoid of plants, animals and the antithesis of a lush tropical ecosystem. Maintaining silence, they navigated their way into the open, lifeless space.

Benito spoke first, "We know they've been here. The

people saw tire tracks all around this area from the grande veículo." Looking down at the ground while walking, he suddenly came across a fresh set of tracks. "Ha, ha, I see them! Here they are!"

The others quickly converged on the spot. "It is just as I thought. These tracks must be from a Mastodon 9000." Capricio ventured with certainty, "They're so wide that it couldn't be anything else. Now, let's see where they lead." With confidence, the foursome spread out across the barren ground.

About five kilometers down the road, or approximately one mile away, the two shady characters were plotting their next move. "We've got to get these charges set so they blast off tonight as planned, Trash! There's no time to waste!"

"Yeah, I know, but why do we always have to do all the hard work... I mean, what about El Presidente and his men gettin' their hands dirty once and a while too?" As usual, Dumpster looked perturbed as he listened to Trasher blather on.

"Look, Trash, we work for GD, not El Presidente, so when we get our orders from the Bossman...we do what we're told and DON'T ask any questions!"

"Alright, I was just wondering, that's all."

"Yeah, well… get to work, or Lucien will have our heads when he gets back!"

"I'd sure like to take a siesta first and get a little snooze before we start setting those charges… whatcha think, Dump... sound good to you?"

"If you don't get off your lazy butt right now…I'll kick you into next week!" Dumpster snarled.

"Man, wow...you're mean! Nobody knows we're here and Lucien won't be back until tomorrow. So, what's the problem?"

"Oh yeah, for your information, Lucien told me Capricio di Leonardis is no longer being held for questioning in connection with the fires. He was released yesterday, you putz! That means he's out there and most likely on our trail right now... get it? We have no time to waste finishing this job!" Dumpster stared at Trasher, arms crossed and looking aggravated. 'What are you waiting for? LET'S GO, DUDE!"

They boarded the Mastodon 9000, fired it right up and sped off down the road. Trasher mused, "Hey, it's pretty cool we get to ride around in this thing. Nice toy the boss gave El Presidente, huh?"

"Sure is… now shut up and drive!" Dumpster raged angrily.

The bumbling henchmen argued among themselves and were oblivious to the fact they were traveling in a direction headed straight for the team. From a short distance away, Capricio and the others caught sight of the behemoth blasting down the road. It was moving fast and recklessly toward their position. "There!" Sequoia exclaimed, "I see it!" They all turned at once in the direction she was pointing and focused their attention on the road ahead, witnessing the enormous Mastodon 9000 approaching in all its massive glory.

"Aha! Finally the proof we need to implicate The

Disturbers as the ones who are setting the fires!" He said, looking over at Benito. This will help us to obtain the evidence we need to clear my name and stop the destruction!"

Juniper asked excitedly, "What's the plan? Are we going to capture the beast?"

Capricio responded coolly, "Yes, J. We are. If we combine our efforts and come at them from various directions, we should be able to surprise them by blocking their escape".

The group fanned out from three sides in an attempt to overtake the hulking UAV, which was proceeding at a rapid speed rate. As the vehicle came closer, Capricio yelled for the girls to clear out of the road so they wouldn't get hurt. "It's going too fast! Get the hell out of there!" Suddenly, without warning, there was a high-pitched, reverberating sound of such profound intensity that the shockwave seemed to come from everywhere. North, south, east and west, the noise bounced off the vehicle, bringing it to a screeching halt. In an instant, the monstrosity was completely shut down. It quivered, quaked, wheezed and sputtered forcefully while loudly convulsing. Odd noises could be heard emanating from under the hood, as if the vehicle was going through death throes.

Capricio turned to Benito, "What was that? Where'd that sound come from?"

Benito pointed to a dense cluster of trees where a familiar face, accompanied by a brace of men, materialized out of nowhere. They emerged silently from their emerald sanctuary. It was Orfeo and the escort he had with him in Rio! Capricio was dumbfounded! How did Orfeo and his men arrive here ahead of the scouting party??? After all, they were traveling on foot and behind them for such a long distance. As the grande veículo lay dormant and dying, made obsolete by mysterious, unseen forces, Capricio waited patiently to ask his friend how he managed to get to this place in advance of them.

Before he could ask, Orfeo replied serenely, "The forest is our home and it speaks to us. It tells us what to do...we come and go here when and where we want. Every time a little more is lost, we suffer. That is why it must be protected."

"Yes, but how did you get here to stop the machine? What was that sound we heard?"

Orfeo smiled peacefully. "We come and go wherever we want in the forest." Capricio and the girls listened in rapt attention and were all amazed by what they'd witnessed. It was nothing short of a miracle. A physical and spatial impossibility that manifested right before their eyes! Capricio knew about telekinesis, which was the practice of using one's mind to move an object and change its matter, but he'd never seen it done before with sound.

Orfeo repeated again, "The forest is our home and it speaks to us."

The hulking Mastodon 9000 lay silent as the grave. The two occupants within were heard audibly disoriented and frantically moving about.

Capricio yelled, "Whoever you are, come out here

right now! You have nowhere to go!" The door slowly creaked open. The foppish thugs stood at attention in the doorway. They held their hands high, "We give up! We don't want any trouble! We're just doing our job surveying the area!" Dumpster yelled back. Capricio instructed them to step out of the vehicle. The two exited cautiously and acted afraid of the tribesman who encircled the behemoth.

Capricio spoke first, "Why are you here...what's the job you're doing? Who are you working for?"

Anxious and distressed, Trasher blurted out, "Lucien, Mr. Higgenbotham, wants us to clear the forest, so the big boss can build a hotel and a golf course."

Dumpster glared intensely at Trasher. "Keep quiet, you fool! Shut your big mouth! We don't know anything and won't talk to anybody unless we have an attorney!"

Capricio replied calmly, "Oh, I think that can be arranged. For now, we've heard enough." Capricio conferred with Orfeo about what to do with the captives. "I'm going to take them back to Manaus to the local Polícia Federal for questioning. I'll remain and give testimony. My friend, I'm trusting you to bring Juniper and Sequoia safely back to the airport so they can catch a flight home, ok?" The two shook hands and gave each other a brotherly hug before departing.

Back in Manaus, Capricio, en route to the police station with Dumpster and Trasher in custody, Orfeo delivered the girls to the airport as promised. While they were waiting for their flight, he thanked them and gave each a tribal talisman to wear for their part in helping to protect the forest.

"We know there will be others who will try to take from us again. This is not over. We will need all the help we can get and would welcome your return when the time comes."

With humility and gratitude, Sequoia replied, "As defenders of sacred forests everywhere, we would be proud to do all we can to protect and preserve your homeland, from any and all, Disturber forces now and always." He gave them both a friendly hug and waved goodbye as the girls boarded the plane.

During the flight, in her usual inquisitive way, Juniper asked, "Why is there so much evil in the world, S.? Why do Disturbers want to destroy such a beautiful place like that, without considering the damage they're causing to people and the environment?"

"I think something inside them is dead, J. They've forgotten the connection we all have to the natural world and how we must cherish that bond. It begins with us, because we're the ones who can make a difference through our actions. We're the lucky ones, too, you know, because we see what must be done to take the action necessary to protect it."

"Thank you, S., for always explaining things to me. It was all so exciting! Such a great adventure! I can't wait to report about everything that has happened to Willow."

"You're right, J. The trip was exciting. I can't wait to get back, too.

"Yeah, I never knew how much I missed the good 'ol

U.S.A! We may travel halfway around the world, but nothing is as sweet as going home, huh, S."

By that time, she had dropped off into a deep, peaceful sleep. Feeling comfortable in the knowledge they had completed a successful mission their first time out, Juniper settled in and snuggled up to her friend for the long ride home.

Chapter 8

The Permafrost Twins

"What good is the warmth of summer, without the cold of winter to give it sweetness." - John Steinbeck

Greenland exists on the extreme northern point of the Earth. It is surrounded by the Arctic Ocean and is in a state of perpetual winter. The landscape glistens in a pristine white glow and is covered by high drifts and vegetation that is heavily laden under a thick blanket of snow. In this cold, desolate place, humans survive precariously, as they do elsewhere in harsh, difficult conditions. In the far north, geographically isolated from the rest of the outside world are people known as the Inuit, who depend on the land and its natural resources for their survival. The Inuit are similar to other tribal cultures in that they remain close and interdependent upon each other. They hunt by themselves or in groups for seal, polar bear and musk ox. They fish for Arctic char and cod, which comprise their main food source. They're unable to grow fruits and vegetables, because arable land is scarce. Farming in Greenland is all but impossible, because it's snow-covered and ice-bound all year round. In the last decade, though, the thawing of the permafrost has exposed more ground and this has increased opportunities for greater sustainability. Since the Inuit survive in large part without local agriculture, their diet consists mainly of protein derived from fish, mammals and other animal sources to hold them over through the long, dark winters.

Additionally, indigenous Greenlanders depend on imports from Denmark and Scandinavia for a variety of items to meet all of their other necessities. The Arctic acts as a unique barometer, because it gauges the health of the tundra biome. It plays a vital role in forecasting climate change. Recent trends, derived from statistical data during scientific expeditions, are pointing toward an upward shift in temperature, as weather patterns are becoming significantly hotter. International climate scientists are interpreting the density of the top layer of snow and the integrity of the permafrost below. These interpretations will help them to make calculations for understanding and predicting the imminent danger degree change will have on global warming. Accumulation of CO2 gases causes The Greenhouse Effect. A rise in the atmospheric temperature is a phenomenon linked directly to man-made carbon emissions around the world. The heat causes environmental degradation and a loss of continuity with the land, which is destructive to the Inuit way of life. It also decreases the habitats for various animal species as well. Over a period of decades, the thaw has exposed deeper layers and slowly released toxic levels of carbon dioxide and methane gas into the atmosphere. It has also opened up the area to agricultural possibilities, which weren't options before. The exposure of the frozen tundra reveals usable land for farming and ranching. It provides the promise of greater self-sufficiency and independence, attracting investments from outside the country. However, this condition presents a quandary. It brings greater economic possibilities from farming, ranching and other land use prospects, while the warming patterns indicate catastrophic events on a global scale.

Temperatures at the North Pole are forcing the glaciers to melt at a greatly accelerated pace, and so, the volume of water in the oceans is also swiftly rising. Estimates from calculations indicate that the sea level will be approximately 1.5 ft. or higher by 2050; this is based on current hotter air temperatures remaining unchanged. The Greenhouse Effect influences the life cycle of animals such as the polar bear, which is significantly essential to the Inuit for food and clothing. The polar bear is inextricably linked to the sea ice and the warmer conditions are directly responsible for the loss of its natural habitat. These environmental conditions have forced the bear to travel farther and farther away to hunt seals, which are their primary food source. Due to melting, thinning, or broken ice floes and the rise in water volume, the bear is being forced to swim extreme distances outside its normal range, unable to find a resting place on the journey, while enduring tremendous physical hardship. The impact on the bear's life is alarming. As an additional consequence of the adult population's struggle in the search to locate food, the young are abandoned and left alone to starve. As the bear numbers dwindle and the glaciers continue to melt at a greatly accelerated rate, the risk of extinction to these and other animals, such as the endangered arctic fox, is likely. These animals will disappear altogether in the near future without intervention. As the risk grows, there is a heightened international awareness, for the demise of this delicate ecosystem is attracting worldwide attention.

Tasiilaq is the most densely populated town located in the southeastern part of Greenland. It is the home to two teenage twin brothers, Inuk and Pan, who were born and raised on the island. The Inuit way of life and its cultural traditions have always been rooted in the environment. Their father, Amaruq, used his native hunting and fishing skills to provide food and clothing for the boys and their mother, Arnaaluk. Considered a good subsistence hunter among his people, Amaruq is passing those abilities on to his sons so that both boys could become capable hunters like their father. They often accompanied him on trips across the vast tundra plain in search of caribou and musk ox. Using implements such as spears, bows and arrows to kill their prey, good hunters can provide for their families with a minimum of difficulty. Pan and Inuk learned, as part of their indigenous heritage, that this way of life was slowly becoming a distant memory. The shifting environmental factors that were impacting their home and creating a new reality based on climate change were all to real. As the CO2 emissions continued to climb, the scientific community raced to the Arctic to study how this contributed to global warming. Scientists eagerly flocked to the top of the world to measure the effects of ice loss. The summer in Greenland was between March and September and measurements were taken at the beginning, and also, at the end of the season. Expeditions were becoming more frequent so that statistical data could be gathered. The objective of these expeditions was to gauge the melting glacial, sea ice and to determine what it meant to the future survival of the planet.

During one such mission that took place in the summer months, Inuk and Pan came in contact with a group of international scientists who were commissioned to do annual measurements on the ice melt and permafrost loss in the Arctic. The expedition boat, Tempus Fugit, was anchored and resting at the mouth of Ammassalik Fjord in the North Atlantic. On board, were three men and two women who were tasked with the goal of measuring the current loss of the permafrost. Weighed down with equipment and dressed from head to toe in warm clothing, they disembarked from the vessel and made their way into Tasiilaq. That day, the boys and their father, Amaruq, were stocking up on supplies at Pilersuisoq, the local supermarket. They were shopping for imported items such as fresh produce, paper products and other goods that were only available at this store.

"Look!" Inuk shouted, "There are some strangers in town!" Pan rushed over to a big picture window that offered a panoramic view of the street to get a better look.

He pointed and then shouted, "There they are! Who are they, Inuk?"

"I don't know, Pan, we'll go find out. Tell Father, let him know where we are going and that we'll wait for him outside." Pan searched for their father in the aisles of the store before locating him in the produce section, squeezing a piece of fruit.

"Ataata, there are strangers in town. Inuk and I want to go see who they are. They're walking up the street right now. Can we go?"

Amaruq replied, "I don't want you two bothering people you don't know. Anyway, they're probably just more scientists coming back to check on the glaciers. It's no big deal. It's okay with me this time, but don't get in their way, okay, that's all. I'll be done here soon and ready to go, so stick close by the store."

"Naturmiik, Ataata! We'll be careful!" Pan rejoined his brother and quickly rushed outside. He was curious to see the visitors. Richard Steffens, the renowned glaciologist from the United States, was walking down the street. He was at the head of the group. It seemed obvious to the boys he was in charge and the leader of the expedition, so they approached him first. Inuk and Pan were not shy. At sixteen years old, they were already young men. A cautious restraint came over them, though, when speaking to an adult stranger who was a foreigner.

Inuk greeted the man, "Halu." Pan offered a similar pleasant greeting.

"Well, hello, nice to meet you both. My name is Richard. I'm a scientist and here to check on the glaciers. During your summer, at this time of year, we measure and study the melting ice. We're comparing measurements taken last year to see what changes have occurred."

Pan replied,"Katigatkit quvianaq", which indicated he was equally pleased to meet the man. Richard recognized the greeting. He had a rudimentary grasp of the Inuktitut language acquired from his many visits to the area in past years.

"I'm pleased to meet you both as well." He said cordially.

Inuk inquired, "Where are you going? Which glacier will you be visiting first?"

"We will go to Apusiaajik first, then to Sermilik. This will keep us busy for the next few days or so."

"May we go along? Pan and I have been watching the glaciers getting smaller and smaller every year. We're very interested in why this is happening."

"This is your home, so I don't see why not. You would be welcome if you can go with us, but only if your father says it's alright, okay? Looking down the street as he spoke, Richard speculated, "And if I'm not mistaken, that stout-looking gentleman trudging toward us must be him."

"Angittuk, I'll ask him," Inuk confirmed as their

father introduced himself. “Ainngai, uvanga Amaruq atira.”

The two men shook hands in a friendly manner as they greeted one another. “My name is Richard Steffens. Very glad to make your acquaintance.” While he spoke, Pan interpreted for the two. As a result, communication went a little smoother. They had received instruction, while at the elementary school from an English speaking teacher, so the language barrier was minimal. Richard continued, “We’re trekking to the Apusiaajik glacier tomorrow morning, and if you can spare the boys, they would be a great addition to our party.”

Inuk and Pan both stared intently into their father’s face as if pleading with him to let them go on a grand excursion to the glacier. Amaruq knew his sons were capable of tracking and hunting caribou, harpooning seals and other game as they had accompanied him on many hunts in the past. They were strong, mature young men, confident in their heritage and knowledgeable in the ways of their culture. Amaruq pondered for a moment before giving his permission for them to go. He considered the request carefully as he looked at the eager expression of anticipation on the faces of his sons. He uttered, “Angittuk.”

The boys were relieved and happy, as was Richard. “Thank you, Amaruq. They will be a big help to us, since they know your country so well.”

Taking his leave, he said goodbye, “Allele, tavvauvutit.” Pan and Amaruq departed and headed in the direction of home, while Inuk stayed behind to make plans for the following day. Richard clarified, "We can meet here tomorrow morning at eight and then take an express boat from Tasiilaq across the Ammassalik Fjord to the glacier."

"Angittuk, we will be here and ready to go. We'll see you then, tavvauvutit." Inuk smiled and waved as he hurried down the street to catch up with his father and Pan.

The summer months in Greenland started in June. During this time of the year, due to the earth's angle to the sun, it did not set. It was a recurring phenomenon and locals were accustomed to it. They called it the midnight sun. It didn't disrupt the sleep pattern of the locals, since it was a normal part of their daily life. Those from the outside, though, were afflicted with acute insomnia.

The following morning, Pan greeted the approaching party with a hearty, "Good morning, ulaakut!"

"Yes, atelihai!" Inuk excitedly called out. Richard and the others sauntered over slowly, gradually coming to where the pair were waiting.

"Good morning." Richard replied wearily. "Thank you both for coming with us today. We'll head out to the jetty and take the charter boat over to the glacier, ok? Ready?"

The boys paid close attention, while walking along with the other members, who introduced themselves on the way. They were a small assortment of climate scientists, consisting of glaciologists and technicians. Richard was the only one who had a modest grasp of the native language, so he spoke for the rest. The annual journey was singularly focused on collecting data to make estimates of the melting ice, permafrost and gauging their effect on the current climate catastrophe that occurs around the world. As insignificant as it seemed, the work was vastly important for predicting future outcomes for the survival of the planet.

Directing his question to Richard, Inuk inquired. “Did you sleep well last night?”

“As a matter of fact, no. The sunlight kept me awake most of the night.”

“Angittuk, we know it’s hard for strangers when they come here. They try to block out the light, but still can feel its energy. The longer you stay, the easier it gets”, reassured Inuk.

“Well, we will only be here for a few days and nights collecting data. So, I’m hoping we get some sleep for at least one of those nights!” The party arrived at the jetty, where a local charter boat was waiting to take them across the fjord. The crossing was relatively easy. It was more of a task, though, to steer around the broken ice floes than navigating straight through, as the warmer air caused the breakdown of the solid ice formations.

As the boat was making its way across, Richard took the opportunity to get to know the boys better. “Have you ever been off this island?” he inquired.

“No, we haven’t. We’ve never been anywhere, not even to Denmark.” Inuk said, while looking at his brother for acknowledgment.

“Don’t you ever want to see what goes on outside of

here? I mean, at your age, there are many places to see and new people to meet."

The two listened intently. They were eager to learn more and curious about the world that lay beyond their homeland. "Tell us, Richard, what it's like?" Pan asked.

"Well, out in the world, climate change has people scared. These days there are more hurricanes, fires, floods, droughts and temperatures at extreme degrees of highs and lows. It's very unstable. Many people don't know what to do. They struggle to find answers. What I've seen that's giving me some hope, though, is young people taking action."

"Angittuk? Who are these young people?" The two mused.

"I know of one group called Willow's Warriors. They're based in America, but travel around the world to protect the planet, protesting against corporations that are polluting and destroying the Earth. They're doing the important work and taking action in the environmental movement."

The boat pulled into the narrow slip and docked. The team disembarked and carried its equipment off as they set foot on the glacier. Poles and ablation stakes were placed during the prior year to gauge the depth of the ice. From these measurements, an interpretation was made to determine the advancement of the melt and further deterioration of the permafrost layer. This was critical to an understanding of climate change and its long-term global consequences. The party trekked over to the ablation zone and located the poles in the snow pit that were placed last year. Since Inuk and Pan were honorary members of the expedition, Richard guided them through the steps of the process and allowed them to take the measurement.

"Use the tape, Pan. Place it next to the pole to take the reading. Measure the distance from the ice to the ground surface."

The boys stepped up to where the pole was installed. With Richard standing by, they took the measurement. Pan exclaimed, "Now, what do we do with it?" A technician marked the spot on the tape measure jotting down the exact inch in a log. Inuk was grateful and expressed his appreciation. "Naturmiik, for letting us help you out today."

"I'm glad you could lend a hand. It's a pleasure to have your company. It's not often a local person takes an interest in what we're doing." At the end of the day, after all the measurements were gathered across different points on the glacier, the team boarded the boat and returned to Tasiilaq. On the way back, the boys' curiosity got the best of them. They wanted to find out more about Willow's Warriors.

"All I can really tell you is that they're a dedicated band of young people who believe in taking action to save the planet."

"We've lived here our whole lives. All the other kids our age are very unhappy. There are no opportunities for adults to work and young people have no social life. Some of our friends have committed suicide. This is our home, but we feel like the polar bear who swims to survive only to drown before it reaches food. We're hopeless here. We want to know more."

In a concerned tone, Richard responded, "If you're really interested in the environmental movement, I can let Willow know. I think she'd welcome the opportunity to talk to you."

"Angittuk, we are for sure!" Inuk declared. "Can you arrange that for us?"

"Yes, I don't see why not. I'll call her tonight, ok?"

"Nakurmiik, Richard" After spending eight hours on the glacier, the team was exhausted. Spending all day in the cold was very draining. However, Inuk and Pan were unfazed, because they were quite accustomed to the freezing climate. As they made their way back to the inn, Richard suggested that they reconnect with him at the same time the following morning. He wanted to let them know how his call with Willow went. They heartily agreed. On the second night, Richard was still feeling the effects of sleep deprivation. However, he made good on his promise and spoke to Willow about the boys. During the call, they discussed the creation of a culturally diverse team of young people from around the world who would work together for the common good of the planet. Willow was clear she felt they would be an excellent addition to the group, as they're indigenous people and have an organic relationship with the natural world. She also indicated that all of their expenses would be completely paid for if they were willing to come to the United States and visit the rest of The Warriors.

"Well, what do you think? Do you think this is something you'd be interested in doing? Joining The Warriors?"

Inuk replied for both, "Yes, it is, but we've never been off our island before. What must we do?"

"There is only one thing to do: ask your father," Richard concluded. 'I must head back out to take more measurements. I'll be at Sermilik, this time and, If you're really interested in joining The Warriors, you can go back with us to the US the day after tomorrow. We have to make a couple more stops along the way, but will arrive there sometime in August."

"You really mean it? You would take us to America!?" Pan exclaimed.

Richard smiled, "Yes, I would. I just hope you won't be too shocked by what you find there after living here all your life."

"Okay, Richard. We will speak to our father today about going with you and we will do our best to convince him."

"Great! Then we will speak again tomorrow morning at the same time. I wish you guys the best of luck!" Swiftly departing, he made a beeline for the jetty to catch a lift across the fjord and catch up with the others.

Inuk and Pan walked slowly back to their house. They were born and raised in Greenland. It was the only place they'd ever known. Leaving here was a scary prospect. They knew it wouldn't be an easy decision for Amaruq to let them go. The boys fretted heavily about what to say and how to explain their interest in getting involved. They thought about how to ask him. He would know they would be sincere if they wanted to be part of something important like saving the planet and making a contribution. But, would he agree to let them go?

Inuk practiced on Pan and used the most determined voice he could muster. He spoke confidently, "We're sixteen years old now, Father. We're grown boys and capable of making good decisions for ourselves. We promise to be smart, to be the way you taught us and we won't get in trouble while we're away."

Pan added, "Yes, and Father, we're both doing very well in our studies with only a year left to go. Since we're off for the summer, we can leave and not miss any school." With their plan of action in place, Inuk and Pan approached the brightly colored wooden cottage where they'd lived their whole lives. They were cautiously optimistic, but apprehensive, since the traditional way had always been to follow cultural norms and listen to their elders.

When they entered the house, Arnaaluk was standing, stirring a pot over an open hearth. Amaruq rested comfortably in the large main room. "Ataata, may we speak to you?"

He replied, "Yes, I'm listening."

Inuk drew a deep breath before clearing his throat. "The time we spent out on the glacier was very interesting. We learned about how important measurements are. They show what's happening here and the effects on the environment around the world."

"Yes, Ataata," Pan added, "I've always wondered

why the glaciers were getting smaller and smaller every year, now I know: it's because of global warming."

"Did Richard teach you those words?" Amaruq inquired. "Scientists are full of facts about other places, but they don't know everything about our home."

Inuk continued, "Yes, he did talk to us about global warming, but our teachers have also spoken to us about why our environment is changing, so we already knew."

Amaruq's expression remained stern, but attentive. "What is it you wish to talk to me about… global warming?"

Pan looked tentatively at Inuk before speaking. "Yes, partly, Ataata, but there is more. Richard told us about a group called Willow's Warriors. They're young people of our age who are environmental activists who stand up for the natural world as we do here. They've invited us to come to America to visit and learn more about what they do."

"We're home from school for another month during summer," Inuk added. "Richard has agreed to take us on their boat to America. They leave tomorrow afternoon."

"What!" Shouted Amaruq. "You have never been away from home! The world outside here is a dangerous place!"

"Please, just consider our request, Ataata. We'd be back before the school year begins. This would be a chance to learn more and meet other young people our age who love the natural world as we do." Both boys implored Amaruq with their words, while showing respect for their father's authority.

Amaruq pondered their request carefully before responding to his expectant sons. "I'll discuss this further with your mother and give you my answer in the morning. Until then, there will be no more talk on the matter."

"Naturmiik, ataata!" Inuk exclaimed. Pan echoed his brother's exuberance, "Yes, ataata!"

Neither of them were able to sleep that night. Tossing and turning, they decided to sit up and talk. "Are you scared, Inuk? If he says no, then we will continue on as we have always done… nothing changes. That's okay, right? Do you think he will agree to let us go? I believe he trusts us enough to know we will be safe."

Inuk wondered, "He needs us here too…but I agree. He trusts us. I hope he'll let us go. After all, it's only for a month."

"Okay, let's try to think positively, relax and get a couple hours of sleep," Pan reassured his brother. Early that following morning, Amaruq was stirring the fire when they came into the main room. He also looked as if he hadn't gotten much sleep, either. Arnaaluk was drinking a cup of tea to take off the morning chill. Amaruq gestured for the boys to sit down. They were transfixed on their father, holding their breath in anticipation, hanging on his every word.

"We've given this some serious thought. It's been our greatest fear that you would someday want to leave this place, especially since you've never been away from here in your life. You wish to go to a strange land and be around people who do not know our ways. This is our biggest concern. We considered this fact, also thinking it would be good for you to learn and see other places to understand them. So, we've decided to allow you to go for one month during your school break."

"Thank you, Ataata and Anaana! We'll be careful while we're in America and we will listen to people, like Richard, who'll look after us."

Arnaaluk asked, "How will you take care of yourselves? We have no money to give you for your trip."

"Willow is the leader of the group and she offered to pay all of our expenses. You don't have to worry about that, Anaana."

"That's very nice. Please thank her for her kindness." Insisted Arnaaluk.

"We will, Anaana." Inuk and Pan hugged their mother and shook their father's hand. "Richard is waiting to meet us at nine, Ataata. May we go see him and share the good news?" Amaruq nodded his head yes and gave his approval.

They arrived at the meeting place as planned. The boys could hardly wait to tell Richard they were going to America with him. They were out of breath from excitement. Pan spoke first. "We can go! Our father has agreed!"

"Yes, it's true!" Inuk confirmed.

"That's great! I'm so happy for you guys. Now, you're officially part of the expedition. We're staying in town this morning to finish up data calculations, then we're making preparations for getting underway this afternoon. The boat is moored at the mouth of the fjord and we'll be leaving from there. I'll expect you two to be ready to go then."

The time went by quickly before departure. Amaruq and Arnaaluk accompanied their sons to the dock to see them off as they boarded the vessel. The goodbyes were solemn and stoic, but heartfelt. The family huddled together, exchanged words of affection and concern for their well-being, which included a promise to return. Richard offered his reassurance and support, adding he would personally look after the boys and deliver them safely to Willow in New York City. Inuk and Pan walked up the gangway and entered the ship. The vessel cast off slowly as it headed down the Ammassalik Fjord and onward toward the Arctic Ocean. The boys stood at the stern, waving goodbye. They shouted "Nagligivaget" happily in unison as they set out venturing forth into the great unknown.

Chapter 9

Mother Earth and Beyond

"Those who contemplate the beauty of the earth find reserves of strength that will endure as long as life lasts." - Rachel Carson

Before the NYC Climate Change rally, Willow felt a strong urge to contact Mother Earth. It seemed as though everything was calming down nicely and running at a more even pace. Oceana and Bill were preparing to return to Rhode Island to spend the cold weather season along the Atlantic seaboard. The Tree Huggers, Juniper and Sequoia, were itching to start a new assignment and The Anti-Fracks were still down in Texas. Willow wanted to discuss future plans for The Warriors as she moved them forward on a path to fulfill their higher purpose. She had a strong need to share some new ideas that couldn't wait. The visit took place at her family home in Kentucky. Willow hadn't shared with her parents the unique connection she'd formed with Mother, as it didn't feel like it was the right time to open up. This unique kind of relationship might not be understood or well accepted. Eventually, once they were ready, sharing with them would come naturally. It was during her junior year of high school that The Oracle first appeared. Her good grades and solid training gained at Kentucky First, provided the opportunity to take a sabbatical from school to start The Warriors. No questions were asked about her plans, just encouragement to be careful. Willow's parents agreed to allow her the opportunity to advance her activism away from home as long as she was properly supervised. They knew she was passionate about the work and committed to become an activist.

The otherworldly nature of this special relationship made the need for privacy of paramount importance. Willow knew it would be relatively easy to slip out of the house for the visit. She always took her faithful dog Ginger, as she would toddle along anyway. Willow went for a walk when she was sure no one would notice. She tried hard to remain hidden from view and stayed a comfortable distance away. In the clear, she summoned the omniscient spirit. "Mother Earth, We Exist!" At the very moment Willow spoke the words, The Oracle emerged, gradually coming into sharper focus. As always, each time she was in Mother's presence, it was totally surreal. It was a sight impossible to describe or rationally explain, supernatural, an extraordinarily divine event to behold. “Hello, Mother! It’s such a pleasure to see you again. I appreciate you coming to talk to me. You’re my guiding light and I seek your wisdom on something of great importance. I’ve been thinking about various ideas for a while now and I wanted to discuss them with you. These ideas… I’m not too sure they make any sense at all. Well, I mean, it’s kinda hard to explain... you understand, don’t you?”

The Oracle nodded in a reassuring way. Willow fidgeted, hesitating to go on, flashing a nervous smile. “I’ve been considering the direction The Warriors are going since we’ve been on this journey. I worry about it daily and am not certain what we must do to move forward. I feel somehow, we need to grow and expand our efforts even further. I’m not sure what else remains to be done, though. I don't know if what we’ve been or are doing is enough, if it’s helping or is it just too little or too late for the planet to make much of a difference. Rowdy says I overthink everything in the extreme and that’s why I stress about little details so much. That sounds about right. My fears and apprehensions are getting the best of me most of the time.” She nervously admitted. “I’ve become so overwhelmed by insecurities these days with all this responsibility. It’s a real drag! Planning can be exciting, yet at the same time, super scary what might happen if we take action.”

Mother’s voice had a dream-like quality as she spoke, “I sense you’re quite concerned, Willow. I know you’re troubled, but that’s simply because of your youth and inexperience in the ways of the world. The task you've been given is an enormous one. However, it's of the greatest importance to undertake as it is part of a larger mission. It requires one to assume immense responsibility for the highest good, which is the protection of the Earth. That's why you were chosen, dear. I recognized in you an authentic heart coupled with great compassion and it's a rare combination for a person at your age. You see the destruction of the planet with pure innocence. You're disappointed and ashamed, heartbroken by all that is cruel and unfair, but also show a conviction to believe and act while following an awakened, spiritual path. This is what moved me to reach out to you those many months ago. I wanted to see if you would take that leap of faith required to clean up the planet." Her voice resonated deeply with an unmistakable kindness and benevolence that was very soothing.

"Oh, Mother, I'm so grateful you selected me for this mission. I fully realize that being chosen to lead The Warriors is the greatest honor and privilege of my life. What we've done so far has given me immense pride. We've been engaged in a struggle to heal our life-giving planet and have carried it out in the spirit of nonviolence. Along the way, we've formed cooperative alliances to promote collective social action and have kept our ultimate goal of raising awareness about the environment as the highest ideal. We honor that commitment by continuing to stand up against Disturber forces around the world; this is our solemn duty to the cause. I've always known in my heart it is the right path to follow, but somehow, now I feel I must do more."

The Oracle replied, "Well, there is considerably more work that must be done, dear. I believe you will find the answers you seek if you look deep inside your heart and truly ask what else can be done. Is there anything else you wish to speak to me about? I sense you want to share what you have in mind. Tell me the next steps you want to take on this journey?"

"Well, Mother. I've imagined many possibilities to grow our efforts and evolve into a movement that will ensure the future well-being of the Earth for many generations to come. I think about this all the time when we're taking a stand and putting ourselves on the line out there. Firstly, I believe we must establish a movement that celebrates life encompassing everyone. We must embrace all of humanity collectively. Years ago, there was a movement called Pro-Life, which became associated negatively with taking away a woman's reproductive rights. I thought about that name and wanted to call ours, The New Pro-Life, as our mission focuses on caring for all life on the planet. We're its stewards and will make healthy choices for generations to come guiding the planet forward toward a strong, stable future. All life matters, not just some…all!"

Mother responded in a calm tone, "Willow, my dear. I feel that's a beautiful and inspired idea. It's a move in the right direction. Sounds altruistic, passionate and I heartily approve. Such a worthy idea to pursue in a time where humanity needs to find a means to embrace every sentient being. The survival of life on the planet depends on it. Is that what you fear? Are you afraid it won't be accepted, somehow?"

"Yes, that's partly true, but more than that, Mother. I'm afraid I won't be able to lead or have the necessary knowledge, ability, or strength of will to undertake such a movement. People won't be open to listen to me since I'm young, female and inexperienced. It's quite a responsibility, considering there's more attention on us now since The Warriors have become so well-known around the world."

"Willow, dear, I must remind you to continue to believe, strive forward and learn to trust yourself. You have a huge capacity far beyond your years for knowing and understanding people, while showing dignity and respect to everyone you encounter. Your intuitive sense of the direction the movement must take, along with help from Rowdy and the rest of The Warriors, will be instrumental in your success. There will be many great changes taking place to guide humanity out of its current darkness. A dire state will get worse before it gets better, as alarm bells are already starting to go off. I can't say more, but a worldwide purge is coming soon. The Warriors will play a vital role in creating awareness, by setting a pragmatic example for others to follow, while healing and restoring the planet over the next ten years. It's going to be a wonderful time to be alive and you will be a big part of it. You will function as a catalyst for positive change."

"Yes, thank you, Mother. But why do you think I can accomplish those goals in the face of so many challenges? Why can't Rowdy be the leader of our group? He's so much stronger than I am. He's a wonderful communicator, fearless and daring to boot!" Willow declared confidently.

Looking intently at her with concern, Mother sighed. "Dear, you're doubting yourself again and underestimating your abilities in the struggle. It's you who's the strong and balanced one. Having leadership qualities doesn't depend on gender for the required work. When you make important decisions, you never hesitate or falter. Even when you're second-guessing yourself, your heart is open and always extended outwards to others in a loving way. What you don't see is how Rowdy looks up to you as the leader of the group. Even though he's brave and capable in other ways, he relies on your tender, compassionate heart to guide and direct The Warriors. When you need me, I'll be there, as always, to support you through the hard times. As the struggle continues in the direction it's going, you will be a rock for others to hold onto. Now, dear, tell me more about your ideas for the New Pro-Life movement."

"Well, Mother, as you know, the first movement held that women weren't capable of making reproductive decisions about their own bodies. That premise didn't honor a women's right to choose or take into account overpopulation as a future concern. We must address the surplus of children who've been abandoned and forgotten who are already here. We must be responsible to not continue to put an additional hardship on the planet. These children need to be nurtured and looked after first. It's my belief, since we're losing animal and plant species around the world daily, with the potential of a mass epic extinction event occurring in my lifetime, to reexamine what it means to respect life fully. Taking into account the needs of all living creatures. In this way, human beings can be the stewards of healthy, thriving ecosystems. They can usher in a new order as a means to guide and prioritize our responsibilities for the survival of the Earth. This is the mission of the movement.

Being a young person in this movement has made it clear that we have almost no voice for initiating change with individuals, corporations and governments. They're unwilling to listen to us. It's only through our protests and lawsuits in an attempt to apply social pressure has it become possible to influence the process. A large portion of the population can't vote until age eighteen in this country and elsewhere around the world not at all. When that time comes, it will be too late to save the planet if it continues on its current, unsustainable course. I feel it's necessary to take further steps to guarantee that young people have a voice and are included in the decision-making process, as our future depends on it. Here in this country, I want to propose a constitutional amendment that will address the concerns of youth. It will allow young people the ability to influence the decision-making process politically. If accepted and ratified, it will establish certain rights for the protection of the environment. These rights will be a safeguard against the threat of ecocide. It's a means of applying pressure, financial and civil, to stop the Disturber forces."

Anxiously waiting for a response, she asked, "What do you think of these ideas so far, Mother?"

Beaming brightly, The Oracle looked upon Willow as any loving parent would their own child. "Whether you realize it or not, my dear, you've made great strides forward during these past two years. All of the engagements that use non-violent means as they combat the evil forces that disrupt nature have been heroic and valiant in the face of major obstacles. I see you developing into a great leader and as someone who is wise well beyond her years, even if she doesn't know it yet. I envision many of your wonderful, ambitious ideas will come to fruition in the near future."

With gratitude, Willow exclaimed, "Oh, Mother, I'll always need your constant understanding, support and steady hand to guide me along this difficult path! Because without it, being a part of this great mission would have been impossible ."

"Thank you, Willow. What you don't realize is you only think you need me. Your insecurities will diminish over time as you begin to understand and believe in your inner strength. That is your superpower, my dear. It has always been there, requiring a little more cultivation to produce the self-confidence that will bring about your wonderful intentions."

"Mother, do you think my ideas are too utopian? My hope for a perfect world in the face of great obstacles?"

"No, not at all. It's what's been needed all along. This planet is a fragile garden. Humans simply forgot how to tend it They've taken without giving anything back for so long that the delicate thread of connection is lost. It was always meant to be a sacred place, from the forests to the oceans. The original people nurtured the Earth with such reverence and care, always maintaining a spiritual connection with other living beings and the land. They held the Earth in high esteem and were in sync with nature. Over a century ago, they had dominion over the Earth when the garden was a vibrant, healthy place. There were Disturber forces around them, too. Sadly, the powers arrayed against them were too strong and the people lost the struggle to protect the natural world. Since that dark time, there has been a steady decline in the health of the planet leading to the current situation the world is in now. Our garden is dying, so something must be done to renew and restore back to its former state, or the planet will not survive. Hope lies with young people, like yourself, tending and caring for the well-being of the planet. You know what you must do to realize this vision and I'll be there with you every step of the way to see it through."

While she listened, Willow felt a rush of abundant light and love, as if she were infused with energy. Mother waved her hand and said goodbye. She gradually disappeared, fading slowly from sight. The seal of approval was given and Willow knew what she must do now to move on these ideas. A meeting of The Warriors was arranged and it was scheduled to take place after the climate change rally in New York City in the fall. It would be a perfect time for most Warriors, but not all of them planned to be there. Willow knew it was important to get everyone's feedback on the Children's Environmental Rights Amendment and to also discuss the idea for the New Pro-Life movement. The gathering would be a perfect opportunity to come together. It would allow each an equal say in the decision-making process and to be a part of creating positive change!

Chapter 10

Arabella

"Where should I go?" - Alice. "That depends on where you want to end up." - The Cheshire Cat in Alice's Adventures in Wonderland

"Father, are you down there? I need to speak to you right away!" The youthful feminine voice had a decidedly stressed tone as it drifted downward from the top floor. It echoed through the large house situated prominently in the Great Neck neighborhood of Long Island, New York, gradually arriving at its intended destination.

He stepped over the threshold of the doorway, methodically ascending the fine mahogany staircase. With one eyebrow raised and a stern, restrained look of disapproval on his face as he entered the bedroom. "Yes, Arabella? What are you shouting about, my dear?"

She spoke while glancing affectionately at him, "Oh, I'm sorry... it's just that, well...I really don't know what to say, Father. When Mother died five years ago, I was sick with grief and pain over her loss, but then you stepped in and have been there for me ever since. You take care of all my needs and wants. I don't know what I would have done without your support. You're my hero, dearest!"

"Bella, when your sainted mother, Arabelle, passed away, I didn't want to go on living. A part of me died that day right along with her." He became increasingly emotional while studying the contours of his daughter's face. "You look so much like her in every way. Her sweet, gentle nature and beauty radiate from you. Everything I do now is with your best interest at heart; everything is for your well-being and your future. Bella, it's all for you, my sweet child. I'm simply not following you. What are you concerned about, dear?"

As she was facing him, attempting to gather her thoughts, pondering carefully what to say, she held back, afraid to tell him how she was feeling. "That is why I'm so troubled, Father. This is hard for me, because I love you so much. Please do your best to understand where I'm coming from, okay? I've been watching the news and what's going on at the Frick and Frack Oil refinery is really upsetting. It's heartbreaking to see the protesters out there putting themselves at great risk to stand up for the environment. When it comes to your business, I remain neutral out of respect for you. I never thought these matters were important to me and felt I shouldn't get involved. I wanted to remain separate from it all. But now, I know that I must listen to my heart and join in the cause with them."

"WHAT! That's enough, Bella." GD roared. "I forbid you to contact them…ever! Those kids are standing in the way of my business ventures. They're creating confusion, causing problems for me wherever I go and are a huge pain in the neck!"

"Please, Father, don't be angry. I need to tell you how I feel in order to be true to myself and follow my heart!" she pleaded.

"Now, Bella…be reasonable! I think for your own good, I'm going to send you back to school…with an escort if necessary! You WILL listen to what I say and obey me. Do you hear? You're MY daughter, not one of those kids running around wild and crazy in the streets!"

"I don't understand, Father. I know they're protesting against the pollution from the refinery… but should there be so much poison in the air that's unhealthy for the people and animals to breathe? Can't something be done to lower the CO2 emissions?"

"ARABELLA! You know nothing about what you're saying! Where did you hear words like that? Who's been filling your head with such stuff!? Stop listening to irresponsible kids who're feeding you a lot of nonsense. We're running a legitimate business, and as such, we operate in the best and cleanest way possible, using the latest technology at our disposal."

"I believe you're being honest with me, Father. But, you see, my generation will inherit this planet and what happens to the Earth now determines the condition it will be in when I become an adult. Can't you understand that, Father?"

"Bella, I don't know who you've been talking to, but everything we do is safe. You have no reason to fear anything. I assure you completely."

"I simply want to find out for myself, be part of the change that's coming and help clean up the planet, Father."

He growled imperiously as he barked orders at her, "Not as long as you live under my roof! You're only fifteen years old and a minor. I'm your parent…you do as I SAY and that's final! You're grounded, young lady! Don't leave this room, as arrangements will be made to send you back to school tomorrow morning."

Begging for sympathy and a little understanding, she said, "I have two weeks left of my summer vacation before school starts! It's too soon for me to go back now!"

GD bellowed, spinning on his heels as he stormed out of the room, slamming the door behind him as he went, "You'll go back when I say so, young lady! It's for your own personal safety… end of discussion!" When the sun rose that next morning, he felt a deep sense of remorse. It gnawed at him and laid claim to his senses. He'd never been in an argument with his daughter before, so the experience was upsetting and oddly disconcerting. After her mother passed, the two formed an extraordinarily close bond of tenderness over their shared sense of grief and loss. It felt secure and unbreakable.

For breakfast, GD had all her favorite foods prepared. Waffles, cantaloupe and a decaffeinated mocha with plenty of whipped cream were specially made. He carried the tray up to her room and gently knocked on the door. "Bella, are you awake, dear? Bella?" The absence of any sound from within struck a deep chord. Nothing could be heard. A pervasive feeling of dread was punctuated by the foreboding silence, which combined with an ominous fear of the unknown. He slowly pushed the door open. His eyes darted around, searching the room for his child. Bella was nowhere to be found. There wasn't a trace of her anywhere. He believed she must have left during the night.

Once the realization sank in that she was missing, GD flew into an instant rage. He hurled the tray against the wall. All of its contents were still warm. Unable to calm down, he yelled out, "Jimmy, where are you!?"

A man's voice could be heard as it echoed down the corridor. He ran hurriedly from the opposite end of the hallway, "Yes sir, I'm coming!"

"My daughter has disappeared! I want a thorough search of the house and the grounds made from top to bottom! I promise you heads will roll if she's not found!"

"Yes, sir! Right away, sir!"

"Thank you, Jimmy. Pardon me for shouting. Help me find her, please." He sniffled as he spoke.

"I understand completely, sir. We will locate your daughter soon, I assure you."

"Thank you again, Jimmy."

Still scanning Bella's room for any sign of her whereabouts, GD caught sight of an envelope peeking out from under the pillow on her bed. As he read the note, a look of surprise and sadness appeared on his face. GD mouthed the words she'd written there aloud. "Dearest Father, I have gone to join the movement. I want to follow in the direction my heart is leading. I hope that someday you'll understand and forgive me for running away. Please know I'm not trying to hurt you on purpose. It's something I must do. I'll call you soon. I love you. Arabella."

As the tears welled up in his eyes, he beat back the urge to cry. He let the paper slip from his fingers and it dropped to the ground. He moaned, "BELLA, WHAT HAVE YOU DONE!?"

She stood in front of the Gardens at the Great Neck Plaza and waited for her cab to arrive. She'd broken into her piggy bank for the journey. It was her private treasure from childhood. All the money saved from weekly allowances and babysitting was used for her getaway. Bella fidgeted nervously while waiting for her ride. This was the first openly defiant act against her father. She was in unfamiliar territory where he was concerned. In the chill of the early morning, The Great Neck Taxi Service pulled to the curb to pick up its passenger. The driver helped Bella inside, then politely asked, "Where to Miss?"

Mustering the confidence to speak, she instructed, "Foley Square New York City, New York, if you please, sir."

"Right, Miss," the driver replied. As the taxi slowly

pulled away, a tinge of sadness, mixed with a sense of excitement, swept over her. Somehow, she intuitively knew there would be nothing to fear, yet that feeling of uneasiness still lingered in the unknown.

GD was unaccustomed to being in a position of disadvantage, so he had trouble coping with the situation. He always had the final say in any business dealings that involved The Disturbers. Those who got in his way were quickly brushed aside, as he was not a man to be trifled with or crossed. While at the house on Long Island, he called Lucien, his attorney, to help formulate a plan to get her back. He was annoyed and perplexed at the events that transpired over the last twenty-four hours and sought his attorney's advice. "I simply don't understand what came over her. Bella has never gone against my wishes before. Why now? Do you think someone from The Warriors coerced her to join them in order to spy on me?"

"No, GD, that's not a likely scenario. I think it's that she's more like Arabelle than you realize or care to remember. Your wife had a gentle nature and a kind heart. Don't you recall how infuriated you'd get when she gave your money away to the homeless since many of them were unable to find affordable housing? Some of them were living in those hovels you own in Bed-Sty. She was so concerned with the poor and those low lifes who rented from you." Lucien replied callously.

Lamenting his loss, GD raised an eyebrow while listening, "Yes, I remember. My dear, departed wife had a kind, but weak heart. I loved her very much, you know.

I'd have done anything for her, given all that I own so that Arabelle never left me."

"Well…I know you did, GD. Now, get a grip on yourself, man, and let's formulate a plan to get Bella back, ok? We know The Warriors are at that rally in NYC along with the rest of those protesters, so my guess is Arabella is making her way to them there. If we enlist the help of the NYPD, we might be able to have that bunch of troublemakers arrested AND get your daughter back!" Lucien crooned, taking pride in his vile ingenuity.

GD's somber, depressed tone was readily apparent. "I'll leave the details up to you, Lucien. But, please, be careful. It's Arabella who's out there amongst those hooligans and she's all I have left, dammit!

"Don't worry, GD. I've got everything completely under control. This may not be the best idea I've come up with lately, but maybe we should get Dumpster and Trasher to check out the scene first and locate her before we take action. They're on your payroll, so we might as well get some use out of them. Not the sharpest tools in the shed, but, nevertheless, handy for our purposes."

"Get on it right away, Lucien! Every moment we waste, I lose a little bit more of her." He said, holding back the tears. "I can't imagine what they might do to her, knowing she's my daughter!"

GD slumped down into his high-back leather easy chair, reminiscing over the past, he let the nostalgia hit him like a tidal wave. *Why did she leave me, Arabelle? I've always given all my love unselfishly to our daughter, just like you gave me.* Groping the air as if reaching out for something or someone, searching desperately through the empty space, he lost control of his emotions and fell to his knees. "Oh, my sweet, Arabelle! You took my heart with you when you left! I'm a broken man! I'll never be whole again, dearest one. Not without you!"

Just then, Jimmy entered the room. "Sir? Is Mr. Higgenbotham here? I heard you speaking to someone and thought he was here."

Wiping the tears from his eyes, GD replied, "No, Jimmy, it was just me… I'm really missing Miss Bella, that's all."

"I understand perfectly, sir. I miss her, too. She reminds me of her mother."

"Yes, Jimmy. I think of myself as the luckiest man to have known her. Is it too late to get Bella back and turn over a new leaf?"

"Never, sir. You can do anything you want if you really put your mind to it."

"Will you drive me to New York City, so we can find our girl, Jimmy?"

"Of course, sir. I'll bring the limo around front. Give me ten minutes."

GD declared,"Thank you, my friend. I feel better already knowing I'm doing the right thing. I can hardly wait to see her again!"

After Lucien set the ball in motion, the two henchmen were dispatched to the scene at the event in NYC. Dumpster and Trasher were lurking in the background, engaged in a mission of deception and mayhem. They attempted to blend into the crowd of young people, which numbered in the thousands. Looking around at the massive assembled throng, Trasher whispered to Dumpster, "What the hell are we doing here, dude?" He sported a disgusted look on his face as he spoke. "Why do you always ask me the same stupid questions every time we get an assignment?"

"Just wondering', that's all. I mean not sayin' anything bad against the boss, but what's he got against these kids? What did they do to him?"

"Listen, Trash. We work for Lucien. He gets his orders from GD and that's all you need to know! Now stay focused on the mission! We're here to look for Bella!"

"Ok! Sorry I asked. Why are you so touchy, dude?"

"Oh, I don't know, let me think… constantly dealing with you?" Dumpster replied sarcastically.

Trash blurted out so loudly that everyone who was within the sound of his voice could hear. "Hey, I think I see her up on the stage… next to the girl with the long brown hair!"

"Yeah, I see her too. That's Willow O'Brien, leader of The Warriors, sitting beside her. I'll let Lucien know. He'll want to get this news right away. You keep an eye on her, Trash, while I go make the call. Don't let her out of your sight!"

"No problem. How hard could it be to keep track of a couple of kids?" responding with a dim-witted expression on his face.

In complete exasperation, Dumpster rolled his eyes. "Stay here and don't move off this spot until I get back!"

He made his way through the crowd, searching for a more secluded place to use his cell phone. "Lucien? Yeah, it's me. We found GD's daughter at the rally, just like you said. She's with Willow O'Brien. What do you want us to do, huh? Snatch her back?"

Before Dumpster could finish his question, Lucien barked, "Be quiet and listen! NO ONE is to interfere with our plans! The boss wants the O'Brien girl taken out, apprehended and arrested. Getting rid of her will throw a monkey wrench into this rally and we'll get Bella back too. Mission accomplished! You and Trash serve one purpose and one purpose only, which is to keep track of her. If there is anything more than that, you two would just get in the way and mess things up! Understand? Now, get back over there and keep an eye on her!"

"Yes, boss! Don't worry. Willow hasn't got a chance in hell!" Dumpster proclaimed confidently. "Boss… are you there? Boss?" The line was dead. Lucien had already hung up, leaving the matter of Willow's fate at the mercy of the unknown and in the hands of the henchman.

Chapter II

The Engagement

"Never doubt that a small group of thoughtful, committed citizens can change the world. Indeed, it is the only thing that ever has." - Margaret Mead

The Warriors were set to attend the NYC climate change rally in early September. Thousands upon thousands of young people from all around the world were on the move. They were coming together making their feelings known, voicing their dissent with the powers that be and the system. Real change was beginning to take shape. Their efforts in many environmental settings were making a difference. Today, promoting divestment in fossil fuels, spotlighting the loss of habitat for animal and avian species as a result of deforestation, lack of clean water availability, the decline of bees and social justice issues, such as poverty, were the focus. The objective of the rally was to have a peaceful protest march, but

The Warriors were bracing for major pushback at the hands of law enforcement, who took their orders directly from Disturber forces.

The others huddled around Willow on the steps of the courthouse at Foley Square, highly stoked for the event and eager to receive their instructions for the day. The group waited impatiently to formulate a plan of action. Situated in Lower Manhattan, Foley Square was the staging area and starting point. Willow brought up possible concerns. “As you all know, we’re here to exchange information about fossil fuels, fracking and to discuss our most recent engagements with Disturber forces at the Frick and Frack oil refinery in Texas. We’ll get our chance to speak at the rally, but the organizers, Josh and Kristin, are well aware that we may be targeted by the cops, so they warned us to be careful. They’ve alerted all participants to take heed and be on the lookout for any trouble.”

“Our top priority, since you’re numero uno on The Disturbers hit list, is to provide you protection, Willow.” Rowdy added, “If they get their hands on you, it would be a huge disaster that none of us could handle…especially me.” He gazed fondly at her, examining each feature in detail as he spoke. Not just their leader, she represented the light and love of his life, having a place of great importance in his heart.

Willow tilted her head downwards. She was reserved and shy, as always. She glanced up at Rowdy and then around at the group. “My good friends, any one of you are as capable as I am to lead The Warriors. All of you must be ready to accept responsibility for the welfare of the rest if I'm not around. We have come so far on this journey. I believe in our mission and have the utmost faith in what we're doing. I couldn't be prouder of each of you than I am right now."

A collective moan emanated from the group. "Oh, no way! I don't agree!" Exclaimed Sequoia. "When we were down in Brazil, you provided the support we needed to get us out of there! Nobody could have helped as you did! We'd NEVER been able to rescue Capricio without Peter's assistance either!"

Juniper wholeheartedly agreed with Sequoia. "Yeah, without your intervention, he would still be stuck in that jail!" The Anti-Fracks concurred in earnest with the girls. The members never doubted her ability to guide and lead. She was the glue that held them together.

Willow was always uncomfortable receiving compliments and thanked everyone for their vote of confidence, quickly proceeding with the informal briefing. "While we're here at the event, our main objective is to stay together and remain safe. It will be easy to get hyped up and get excited or angry while feeling inspired to act. There will be people marching in the crowd, at the back and sides; they're here to keep folks safe from police and counter-protesters. Police are looking for agitators and anyone who tries to destroy property; the news media calls these people "looters." They will be targeted and the cops are going to make arrests, so we must be careful. This is a peaceful rally and we're marching to protest the destruction of the environment at the hands of

Disturber forces. We must expect difficulties and be ready, as anything is possible. It's important for us to look out for each other today."

All at once, Josh and Kristin showed up to the group in an excited state. "Hey, wow. We've been looking all over for you guys!" Exclaimed Kristin.

Josh added, "Yeah, someone is really trying to find you, Willow."

"Oh, yeah." She said quizzically. "Who could that be?"

"Well, from her looks, she's just a kid of about fourteen or fifteen. The girl said she knows you. Pretty pushy about it too." Josh shrugged his shoulders. "She seems harmless enough. Her name is Arabella. Does that sound familiar?"

"Hmm, nope, not sure." Willow asked, "Where is she?"

"She's waiting at the organizer's booth. I'll take you over to her right now."

Kristin walked Willow to the event kiosk, where everything was starting to come together and Arabella was waiting. Josh stayed behind with Rowdy and the rest to provide instruction, making further preparations for the day's activities.

When they arrived at the staging area, Arabella could hardly contain herself. She bolted, running like a wide-eyed filly toward the freedom of an open pasture, making a beeline for Willow. She was excited, panting heavily and extremely animated, behaving as if she were meeting a celebrity. Bella asked, "Are you, Willow?"

"Yes, and who might you be?"

"Oh, my goodness!" She exclaimed. "I've been trying to track you down! I thought you might be here! My name is Arabella. I think you know my father… GD? He owns the Frick and Frack oil refinery in Texas."

Looking stunned and amazed, Willow inquired, "Uh, yes, I'm well aware of who he is. Where is your father now? Does he know you're here?"

"Yes, I believe he does. If not, he is more than capable of finding me. I told him I was going to join The Warriors, so I imagine he's really upset with me right about now."

Willow pondered for a moment and felt a bit confused. Could there be an ulterior motive for her being here? Disturber forces would do anything to spy on them and infiltrate their ranks in any devious way possible. She didn't put anything past them. Yes, but would the leader of such a corrupt organization go so far as to send his own daughter here to carry out that plan? It was mind-boggling attempting to figure out all the various angles. They were in more than a bit of a quandary. Willow knew from past experience Disturbers were capable of anything and to stay cool no matter how strange things looked.

"Mmm hmm, I see. So, what do you want? To join The Warriors?" Bella vigorously nodded her head. "Let me give you some history. We're a small band of dedicated activists. Each person has a very unique talent that they bring to the group. What special skills do you have to contribute?"

"Well, I'm not sure. I've never really done anything like this before. I only know that I want to become a Warrior like you!" Bella replied confidently.

"Ok, only time will tell. It takes more than just curiosity to become a Warrior. You must be able to offer something useful to benefit the group. Alright. For now, you can follow me. We'll head back and I'll introduce you to the rest of the group."

Bella gushed, "Really? You mean it? Great! I can hardly wait!"

They returned together to the meeting place. As the two approached, Rowdy came up to greet them.

"Willow, Josh is telling us that we need to dress in all black. We need to cover our skin, tattoos, hair, etc. to protect against potential charges that could be filed later to identify us on social media. He says to take these precautions in case we get arrested. Who do you have with you?"

"Rowdy, would you please get the others?" She asked sweetly.

He examined Bella as he replied in a slow, Texas drawl, "Of course. I'll go get 'em right now."

The young women looked for a place to sit down and made themselves comfortable on the steps leading up to the entrance of the courthouse at Foley Square. The rally was still more than two hours away from starting and there weren't many others around at the time. Still feeling nervous about Bella's sudden appearance at the event, Willow inquired, "Tell me more about what you know of The Warriors and what inspired you to want to become an activist?"

"I have been following the deeds of The Warriors for a couple years. I admire what you're doing, standing up for the environment and the young people being so brave. What you all do inspires and motivates me to be a better person."

Willow paused for a moment impressed with Bella's frankness. She chose her words carefully before speaking. "We're committed to protecting the planet. Each of The Warriors has a duty to safeguard it at all costs. There is no higher purpose than that for us to fulfill." Bella bubbled over with enthusiastic approval. She could barely contain herself while listening to Willow speak. "The biosphere is dying. It's our job to respond to this crisis wherever Disturber forces are exploiting and damaging the environment. We're guided spiritually in these actions as well."

Bella inquired, "Who're these Disturber forces?"

Willow stated emphatically, "They're individuals and organizations who use the environment as a way to make money for selfish reasons, without a concern for the harm they're causing. The results are disastrous and all so they can make a profit. Our responsibility is to engage them in 'hot spots' around the world. This is where they operate. We utilize any legitimate means at our disposal to stop their activities." She glanced out across the courtyard and saw a familiar sight coming through the sparse crowd. "Ah, here they are."

Julian and Donald were out front. "Hey, Willow!

Where'd you go for so long? We've got some great ideas for the march. I think we ought to walk against traffic to get people to stop and take notice of the message we're sending. What do you think?" Julian asked.

Before Willow could answer, she noticed something strange. Donald was stopped dead in his tracks, as if struck by a bolt of lightning. He couldn't take his eyes off their guest. "Oh, I want you all to meet Bella. She is GD's daughter. She came here specifically to find out more about us and possibly join The Warriors."

Willow looked perplexed as she glanced over and asked Donald if he was feeling alright. Donald stood still, transfixed on Bella. Julian got toe to toe with his friend. "Hey, buddy…what's the matter? I don't think I've ever seen you like this before…you ok, bro?"

Donald slowly snapped out of his trance. He'd glimpsed a bit of heaven and wondered what solar system she'd come from. Nothing so divine in human form ever existed on this planet before. His feet were firmly on the ground again as he stuttered, "Oh, whe...whe...where are my manners?" He nervously offered his hand in friendship. "Hi, my name is Donald."

Looking directly at the assembled group, she said, "It's a pleasure to meet you."

Julian shook his head from side to side while watching his friend. He muttered to himself, "Oh, no, this can't be happening again! First, Rowdy falls head over heels in love with Willow, and now, Donald is dopey for this kid! Hmm, why doesn't someone fall in love with me? I'm not a bad-looking guy. What's wrong with me?!"

Each of The Warriors took turns introducing themselves. They were friendly and cordial to Bella. They welcomed her and shared a kind word.

Juniper was the lone holdout. "Hey, wait a minute… your father is the boss man of The Disturbers…what are YOU doing here!?"

Bella felt herself trembling as she replied, "Um, yes, that's true, but you don't know him like I do. He's kind, generous, very dear to my heart and I love him."

Juniper blasted back in anger, "You've got to be kidding! The leader of The Disturbers? Kind and generous? Not by my count! You've had everything given to you, while we've always had it rough! You don't belong here!"

Bella was noticeably upset and crying by this time. Her immaturity showed and she quickly became overcome with emotions. Sequoia urged Juniper to calm down and hold her tongue. After all, Bella was not her father and, therefore, not responsible or accountable for his actions.

Donald stepped forward like a perfect gentleman and reassured her. He displayed a tender side that was not often seen. He smiled and said in a comforting voice, "Don't worry, Bella. It's alright. You're welcome here anytime. You'll be safe with us." The rest of the group, Julian in particular, observed the encounter with fascination. Donald had always been a devoted, dependable and loyal friend who was committed to the work. He was eighteen and up to that very moment, had shown little to no interest in girls. None of them had ever witnessed this behavior before.

Willow advised, "Now that introductions have been made, we must get on with the business at hand." She gave a quick glance in Juniper's direction as she spoke.

Rowdy cautioned, "Willow, my greatest concern is for your safety. We must be on the lookout for the cops and for those two Disturber henchmen, Dumpster and Trasher, who might be hanging around and waiting for an opportunity to strike."

Looking at him fondly, she replied, "That's true…we must keep a watchful eye out for each other today. I think we will move together in pairs. Each one will be responsible for the other. Since Bella is here as our guest, I'll take her with me." Once Bella heard she was going to be spending the day with Willow, her mood instantly improved.

Behaving like a giddy schoolgirl, she gushed, "Oh, do you mean it? I promise to stay right by your side. You won't have to worry about me!"

Willow chuckled to herself. "No…I don't think so, Bella. You appear to have a good head on your shoulders."

Donald abruptly reacted to the pairing assignments. "Willow, don't you think it might be a better idea if the boys looked out for the girls? I can take care of our guest. You and Rowdy could be together, and Julian will look after Sequoia and Juniper."

Willow replied firmly, "No, we're all seasoned

Warriors. We're capable of standing up for ourselves and protecting one another, regardless of gender. That's a nice try, Donald, but Bella stays with me."

In the lull before the start of the rally, Donald made a point of getting to know her better. "Bella…is that short for something?" Donald inquired.

"Yes, Arabella. I'm named after my mother, Arabelle. She died five years ago, when I was ten. Her loss crushed me deeply. She was my dearest friend, closest confidante and constant companion, while my father was away working."

"I'm so sorry to hear that. It must have been terrible to lose your mother at such a young age." Donald replied compassionately.

"Yes, it was. I don't think I'll ever really get over it. My father supported me and was there through thick and thin. He's my hero."

Donald sat back. He thought quietly to himself, carefully choosing his next words before speaking. "We're committed to protecting the planet from those who want to destroy it. This mission takes us around the world on engagements standing up to Disturber forces. I don't know why your father chose the path he's on. He's playing a big role in the destruction of the planet and I believe his actions are wrong."

"Yes, I agree, Donald. That's why I left home to come here. We had an argument about what was going on at his oil refinery in Texas. The pollution is harmful for people to breathe. I said that I admired The Warriors for their bravery and wanted to be part of the movement too. He got very angry at me. It frightened me so much, that I decided to leave."

"Bella, I think you're a very courageous person and I'm glad that I met you."

She smiled shyly while looking at Donald. She'd never known affection from an individual other than her father. Their newfound friendship was suddenly interrupted by the appearance of Willow.

"Come on, you two. The rally is starting! Bella, you go with me. Donald, join The Anti-Fracks. We'll all meet up somewhere in the middle."

Donald helped Bella to her feet. "Stay close to Willow. She's not just our leader, but will teach you about the environmental crisis too."

"Oh, I will. I'm so proud to be here today and especially to meet you, Donald. I know I'm lucky to have this opportunity and I won't waste it."

"I believe you'll do fine, Bella," Donald said, looking back over his shoulder as he walked away.

The event started just before noon. Willow was scheduled to speak within the first hour. Rowdy and The Anti-Fracks took up strategic positions around the venue to act as advanced guards. Their sole job was to protect her. Bella followed Willow's instructions to the letter and stuck close by her side, even while she was on stage preparing to address the assemblage.

Willow waited to be introduced. She was deep in thought about what she wanted to say. She was dressed in a paisley print top and a peasant skirt, that harkened back to another era, one where peace, love and questioning authority ruled the day. Her mind began to wander. What had changed so radically back then to motivate a generation to act? Were their values so completely different from ours? They were protesting against an endless war that was halfway around the world. Nobody knew why it was being fought. It was the same as today. That generation was anti-establishment too. It stood up to corrupt, greedy individuals and corporations who were exploiting the planet, while droves of counter-culture revolutionaries were reconnecting with the land, heading toward a simpler life. They had the right idea, but what went wrong? A tug on her sleeve snapped her back into the reality of the present moment. "Willow! They're calling for you to come up to the microphone!" Bella exclaimed.

Willow glanced over to where Kristin was standing. She was frantically waving for her to come forward. Willow rose quickly, straightening her outfit. She walked briskly to the platform. The throng of young people that crowded in the square quieted down some before Willow began speaking. They were youth from all across the country who had dredged up the courage to act and were determined to make a difference. Each of the speakers was introduced by the topics they were scheduled to discuss. Willow planned to speak on fracking and divestment in fossil fuels.

Kristin attempted to calm down the boisterous crowd. "Quiet, please! Let's be quiet, people! Our next speaker is someone who is at the forefront of the environmental movement. She and her group, The Warriors, are active around the world and stand up for the cause wherever they go." The crowd broke into a thunderous applause. "Welcome, people…Ms. Willow O'Brien!"

"Good afternoon, everyone. It's very encouraging to see so many hopeful faces here today. Faces of those who are willing and ready to do what's necessary to address the climate crisis. We're the ones who must direct this change and who must educate those adults in power about what is at stake. With your voices and efforts, we will make known the dire condition the planet is in, so that our cause will be heard!" The cheers and applause resounded loudly, echoing across the courtyard. "The Warriors have been busy over the past few years. We've been confronting hurricanes, fires and the oil industry here and abroad. Most recently, though, we've engaged with Disturber forces at the Frick and Frack Oil Refinery in the Texas Panhandle. Our protests over the noxious gas emissions and other contaminants in the air and water were effective in shedding light on the problem. Making the public aware of fracking as an unstable process that is linked not only to chemical pollution of groundwater, but also to earthquake activity due to destabilization. We will continue to push for divestment in fossil fuels and discourage the purchase of gas-guzzling vehicles such as: the Triceratops 4000, the T-Rex 5000 and the huge Mastodon 9000 made by the Disturber company, Forensic Motors. We're all under some sort of hardship, and as a result, dependent on this Earth for the life it provides, the food we eat and medicines for healing. None of us, not one, will be spared the devastation that follows the collapse of the Earth's ecosystems. We're integrally linked together for our survival. Right now, we're on a great mission. We're all taking direct action to clean up the planet. It's our honor to participate with young people, here and around the world, who want to do this important, purposeful work."

After a rousing applause, Willow took her seat next to Bella. "Well, what did you think? How'd I do?"

"Oh, I'm so impressed with you, Willow! To listen to you speak with such conviction and strength of character… you're the bravest person I've ever met!"

"Thank you, Bella. I see great strength in you too. It takes courage to come here against your father's wishes. When the march starts, I want you to stay close to me for safety."

"Don't worry. I never want to leave your side!" Bella proclaimed proudly.

A half-hour later, the crowd began to march from Foley Square to Battery Park. They were inspired and stimulated by what they heard. The spirit of revolution was on full display for all to see. The NYPD lined either side of the street. They were arrayed in full tactical riot gear, flanking the sea of protestors and ready to forcibly engage at a moment's notice.

Dumpster and Trasher went incognito and undercover, swept up and blending into the fray, moving through the street with the rest of the crowd.

"Lucien ordered us to watch for Willow and tip off the police when we see her. Ok, Trash?"

"Wow, look at all these crazy kids! I don't get why

they're protesting against the boss, Dump. What did he do to them, huh?"

"They're just a bunch of troublemakers. That's all you need to know, dude. Don't make me look bad this time, ok…try to do your job!"

"Ok, whatever. No sweat, Dump. How hard can it be to find those two girls anyway?"

"Oh, I don't know…in this crowd…maybe impossible, you fool! Keep a lookout, Trash!"

"Oh yeah, impossible, huh? Guess what? I see her over there!" He pointed in the general direction of an entourage of young people who were linking arms and holding up signs demanding fossil fuel divestment. There was Willow and Bella. Trash puffed out his chest, "See, I told you… no sweat!"

"Alright! Don't lose sight of them while I go find one of the NYPD's finest." Dumpster hurried in the direction of the police line. He pushed and shoved people out of his way. The peaceful protest march proceeded smoothly and in an orderly, non-violent fashion. There was no rioting. The participant's goal was to raise awareness through the agency of positive change. There was a prior mandate that no outbreaks of aggression were to take place. Protesters held signs displaying messages, such as: "Divestment equals freedom from oil dependency", "The Earth is our birthright, it isn't for sale!" and "Frack Off!" As the crowd approached Fulton Street, officers were waiting to halt their progress and cause delays. Rowdy, Sequoia and Juniper pushed their way through the crowd to get to where Willow and Bella were standing. Rowdy stood firmly in front of the two women. His arms were extended outward in a defiant stance and his body placed a protective shield around them. One of the officers approached, indicating he was only interested in Willow and that she was under arrest for inciting a riot.

Instantly, Rowdy went ballistic. "What? Hell no, you can't have her! You'll have to go through me first!"

Sequoia and Juniper burst in, "If you take her, you might as well take us too!"

"No, Rowdy, stay back!" Willow pleaded as she looked at him lovingly. "We stand for non-violence. Responding in anger toward others is not our way. Please take care of the group, dear, and get Sequoia and Juniper out of here. I'll be alright. Continue marching, as planned, with the goals we set in place."

Donald and Julian restrained Rowdy as a female officer escorted Willow to a waiting patrol car. She said one last thing as calmly as possible; it was to look after Bella and call Peter while she waved goodbye.

Chapter 12

The Light at the End of the Tunnel

"Everyone thinks of changing the world, but no one thinks of changing himself." - Leo Tolstoy

Peter entered the building with all the storied presence and panache of a well-known litigator. The effect was like Moses parting the Red Sea. His reputation cleared a path and garnered great respect from those who recognized him. With far less fanfare, Rowdy accompanied him into the building staying close by his side. The desk sergeant at the 5th Precinct was equally impressed as Peter approached the counter. He bellowed, "Where are you holding Ms. Willow O'Brien? I'm her attorney and I demand to see her!"

"Yes, Mr. Kensington, I know who you are. She was brought here a few hours ago and is being held for inciting a riot. You may go in and visit her now if you like."

He glared at the sergeant as he spoke in an impatient, assertive tone, "Yes, I wish to see her right away!" Peter instructed Rowdy to wait in the reception area and assured him he would try to arrange a visit to see her afterward.

He found Willow in confinement. She was sitting comfortably and looking relaxed. She stood up quickly and smiled cheerfully in anticipation of his arrival. "Oh, I'm so glad to see you… I knew you'd come, my friend."

"Willow, this is not the place I expected to see you on a visit to New York City. I thought I'd hear about the outcome of this trip as a great victory in raising awareness for the cause."

"Oh, but Peter, it has been a success. It was clear at the rally that people of all stripes are more aware. They see the divides that exist, the inequities between races, classes, genders and all facets of society. We're shining a light on the environmental crisis and the need for a response from all members of society. The declining health of the planet is a direct reflection on humanity's failure to protect each other, our home and the inability to collectively evolve as a species."

"You know I'm sold. However, it's my job to get you out of here, ok? This is where I come in, right? The charge they're holding you on is bogus. The event was well organized and free of any incident. This was an attempt to get you out of the way and to stop you from being a part of the rally. It will be easy to establish that fact and get the charge dropped as there were many witnesses." In an attempt to bolster her spirits Peter added, “There is also a young man who is worried sick about you and waiting out front. Should I go get him now?”

There was a distinct hint of hesitation in her voice that was readily apparent as she spoke. “Alright, Peter, I guess you should. We can’t keep him waiting forever.”

“I don’t understand, Willow. You do want to see Rowdy, don’t you?”

She blinked away the tears and swallowed hard. “We’re so young, Peter. My feelings for him, considering all that’s going on, scares me. The thought of something bad happening to him out there keeps me in a constant state of fear. When they arrested me, Rowdy tried to fight them off with his bare hands! I was so relieved when he stopped, after I pleaded with him to stay out of it. I know it was hard for him to let me go.”

“Willow, this is none of my business. The last thing I want to do is give relationship advice, but the two of you love each other. Even an old guy like me can see that. Your combined efforts are the driving force behind The Warriors. It’s the perfect balance; like yin and yang. Together is where you get your strength. I admire you both for your commitment and dedication to the cause. It’s very inspiring.”

“Thank you, Peter. Your wise counsel constantly reassures me. It means a lot. Yes, would you please go get Rowdy now? I do want to see him.”

Giving her a thumbs up while taking his leave, Peter added, “Anytime, Ms. O’Brien.”

A short while later, Rowdy appeared, escorted by a

guard. Looking concerned and worried, he asked, "Are you alright? They didn't hurt you, did they?"

"No, I'm fine. I just talked to Peter and I shouldn't be here much longer."

Rowdy leaned against the bars of the cell and reached in to touch her and hold hands.

The guard step forward and interrupted their visit ordering the couple to stop. "There is no contact allowed! Back away from the cell door!"

"Yes, Rowdy… it's better this way with the bars between us, as I have something to say to you." Willow gained her composure, while carefully choosing the words as she tentatively spoke. "When we first met, I didn't believe that this kind of love was possible. It was too much to imagine that a beautiful man might ever think of me as someone special. Then when I realized that you felt those same tender, deep feelings I had, I knew I didn't just care for you, I needed and wanted this love in my life. You're the perfect reflection, mirroring all the shadow and light of my soul. Your feet are always on the ground, while you reach for the highest good. Like the earth below and the sky above." Her eyes welled up with tears as she continued, "I can't do this work without you. I might as well stop now and call it quits. Your strength is the energy that sustains me. When I run too fast, you catch me before I fall. You help me stand up for what I believe in, follow the path and stay true to the mission. All of it means nothing without you, Rowdy."

He knew at that moment she was his one true love.

She was out of reach, looking for reassurance in the comfort of his loving arms and helpless to physically reciprocate her love. He caught his breath, "You've never spoken to me like this before. I don't know what to say. I'm a man of few words. As I stand here looking at you behind bars, I know I'll never feel for anyone the way I do for you. Try shaking yourself free of me if you can, girl! I'm not going anywhere without you, love! You're stuck with me for life!"

Willow trembled hearing Rowdy's words. He'd always spoken his mind about the mission, but he kept his emotions well hidden in matters of the heart. His overt display of affection was so moving she was incapable of doing little else but cry.

"Willow, my dearest, please don't cry. I don't want to be the reason you're unhappy."

"Oh no, my love, these are not tears of sadness, they are tears of joy! Forgive me for ever doubting you!" Rowdy leaned against the bars in a vain attempt to reach her, but was swiftly reprimanded by the guard. He was hot with anger, but held his temper. He scowled, "I'm going to find Peter so he can get you out of here right now!"

"Wait, Rowdy! Don't go. Please stay a little longer!" He departed so quickly with the guard following him closely as he walked briskly down the hallway oblivious to her request.

As soon as Rowdy entered the reception area, he spied Lucien Higgenbotham. "What's HE doing here!"

Pointing in the direction of the sinister figure with the gargoyle-like features.

Peter quickly stepped in between grabbing Rowdy by the shoulders. "Wait a minute, son! The only reason Lucien is here is because GD's daughter, Bella, is missing."

"Peter, I want her released right now! She doesn't belong in this place! If you can't do it through legal channels, I'll get her out some other way! I knew The Disturbers were behind Willow's arrest. Otherwise, why would HE be here?" Pointing to Lucien again as he spoke.

"Calm down, Rowdy! Losing your cool won't get her out any faster!" Peter implored.

Grinning like a devil, Lucien licked his lips as he watched Rowdy have a meltdown. "Seems like you have a little problem, huh? You've got something we want, and we've got something you want…quite an interesting dilemma." Rowdy lunged at Lucien with clenched fists, temper flaring out of control.

Peter narrowly succeeded, managing to wedge himself between them just in the nick of time. "Get a grip on yourself, young man! This is not helping Willow, you know." Peter reasoned, patting him on the back. "She wouldn't want you to react with violence. Besides that, you could get yourself in a lot of trouble. We'll find a way to get her out, ok? Why don't you wait outside until we come to an agreement."

Still agitated and upset, Rowdy stormed out without

saying a word. Peter turned to Lucien and asked dryly, "Now, what do you want?"

"We've already got what we want. That troublemaker, Willow, is off the streets and behind bars. What we want is Bella. An exchange of prisoners is what we want. GD thinks Willow has brainwashed her against him and that he'll never see his daughter again. I told him she wouldn't be so stupid as to follow The Warriors. Bella's got more sense than that."

"Don't be too sure, Lucien. These young people are committed to saving the Earth. It's their inheritance they're protecting. Bella is at that age where she's questioning authority and her father is no exception. The more he tightens his grip, the more she'll slip through his fingers."

Lucien responded snappishly, "You and those do-gooders think whatever you like, but GD is sending her back to boarding school for good! She'll never be able to run away from him again!"

Just as their discussion was becoming more heated, rising to a fever pitch, the door of the precinct swung wide open and Rowdy, Bella and Donald walked in. Bella approached Lucien with a fretful, concerned look on her face. "Why have you had Willow arrested? Is it because of me? Don't take my actions out on her!"

Donald approached Bella from behind and calmly consoled her. "Don't let this upset you, dear. We'll protect you."

"Dear!" Lucien bellowed. "What goes on here? You're only fifteen years old, young lady! GD will blow a gasket when he finds out you're socializing with this strange boy!"

Bella looked affectionately at Donald, then replied. "He's not strange. I have known real kindness here and felt a sense of belonging with The Warriors. They've welcomed me with open arms and I'm truly grateful for their friendship. I hope it will last a lifetime! I'm staying with them until Willow is released!"

"I simply don't recognize you anymore, Bella. I'm starting to believe what GD said was true. The Warriors have brainwashed you!"

"Don't be ridiculous! Let Willow go, or I'm never coming back home!" Bella's righteous indignation brimmed over and her revolutionary spirit was on full display.

Donald watched with obvious admiration. He thought that if Willow could see Bella now, it would be easy to tell she had the stuff Warriors are made of.

Peter pressed hard for an answer. "Okay, Lucien, the young lady has spoken. We need to get this situation resolved right now… do we have a deal?"

Lucien looked slightly dejected, as he so loved a good fight. He sauntered over to the desk slowly. "Yeah, it seems like we do. Sergeant, the charges against Ms. O'Brien… I want them dropped and her released."

"Yes, Mr. Higgenbotham, I'll take care of it right away."

"Bella, get your things. Let's go. Your father's waiting."

"Not until Willow is safely free and back on the

street. I'll call Father as soon as she's out. Then, we'll talk." Bella beamed confidently while looking in Donald's general direction.

"I'll convey your message, although rest assured, he won't like it." Lucien said, scoffing at her remarks.

Later that same day, Rowdy, Bella and the others waited patiently outside the precinct for Willow's release. Willow emerged with Peter and looked relieved to see the light of day. She eagerly wanted to reunite with The Warriors. The group encircled her in an energetic swirl of happiness. They were overjoyed, but none more so than Rowdy. He held her close. While drawing a breath, he whispered in her ear, "I need you in my life. I'm hardwired to love you, no matter who or what comes between us."

"I love you too." Her heart was pounding and her pulse racing when she looked deep into his eyes. "You're my rescuer and my bright, shining hero."

"I'm glad you're back where you belong… with us." Kissing her as he spoke.

Bella interrupted their tender reunion and stepped in between them. "Okay, you two… save it for later. Are you ready to get back to work? If so, this is my plan. Little does my father know that my path is moving forward in a different direction. I can't leave him right now. He has depended on me entirely for a closeness, since mother's passing. I realize he will never voluntarily listen to you about the cause, unless he thinks I'm going to stay with The Warriors. His need to get me back is what will force him to talk to you, Willow."

Willow took her time to respond thoughtfully, urging Bella to reconsider what she was suggesting. "Bella, it's important you understand that your father may take your disobedience as the ultimate threat to his authority. Your life may change in radical ways as a result, and you may lose your freedom altogether."

"Yes, I'm aware of that. His actions made it clear that he wants complete control over me. You may not think he's much of a human being since your encounters with The Disturbers have been so negative and hostile, but he's still my father and I love him."

"I respect that and applaud your courage, Bella. When the time comes, we welcome you with open arms as a member of the team."

"Really? Do you mean you think I've got what it takes to be a Warrior?"

Willow nodded her head yes, and replied, "You're making a strong start and I think I'm a good judge of character." She winked at Donald as she spoke.

"Thank you so much! Now, let me call him and set up the meeting, ok?"

As Bella looked around at Sequoia, Juniper, Donald, Rowdy and Julian, the tears began to flow. "You guys are so special to me. Each one is loyal to the other and dedicated to the cause. You're a fearless band of heroes!" The rest of The Warriors gathered around in the spirit of camaraderie and made it clear they all approved of her.

Bella contacted her father to set up the meeting. When she called, he was driving into Manhattan via the Queensboro Bridge. She was pleasantly surprised to hear he was so close. She was reassured to know he was on his way and acting out of fatherly concern for her welfare.

In the fifteen minutes prior to GD's arrival, Willow pondered what she'd say to him. He'd been more than just a disturber of the environment who had created havoc and destruction in his wake; he had made his decisions with callous disdain. He'd shown no concern for the harm they'd caused to others. His only motivation is driven by greed in the pursuit of money. And what about Bella? She was just beginning to see the light. She was learning to trust her instincts and follow her heart. If Willow criticized GD, this might result in Bella questioning her feelings about the cause. Willow knew it was critical to ultimately honor the commitment made to Mother Earth. That every engagement of The Warriors reflect the highest purpose; the protection of the planet. It had to be imparted in what she said and believed about the movement. The message today had to be clear and concise.

The meeting was to be held in a public place. Battery Park was the mutually agreed upon location because it was close to the precinct and easily accessible. The two young women waited patiently. Bella's nerves were on edge. She was worried about how things would go. "I know what you must think of my father, but he's a businessman and not an evil monster. Please give him the benefit of the doubt, Willow, for my sake."

"I intend to, Bella, especially for your sake. We've encountered Disturber forces on many engagements before. It's clear their actions are misguided. Their decision-making is driven by the desire for money and power. Mother believes that their kind must go the way of the dinosaur if humanity is to survive. A big part of our purpose is to educate people by showing them how to move forward out of the old ways and into the new."

Bella asked inquisitively, "Who is Mother?"

"Hopefully, one day, I'll be able to tell you. For now, know that she's our guide."

The stretch limousine turned onto West Street, heading toward their meeting place. Bella saw the car approaching and excitedly ran to meet it. Jimmy brought the vehicle to a full stop, put it in park and then hurriedly got out to open the door for GD. He exited the vehicle with an air of superiority, rank and privilege. His attitude was dictatorial and readily apparent. Bella ran to greet him and the two hugged as if they'd been separated by more than just time and space. "Oh, Father, I missed you! Do you forgive me for running away?"

"Yes, dear… I missed you too. I don't understand why you ran away… am I not good to you? Don't I give you everything you want?" He asked.

"It has nothing to do with you, Father. I needed to find out some things for myself. That's all. Let me introduce you to Willow. She's looking forward to meeting you."

They walked over, arm and arm, to the park bench where Willow was sitting. The sight of seeing GD in a more humanistic light was a bit odd, but refreshing. It was a hopeful sign that the meeting would go well and be a success. Bella was correct in her estimation that he would be more approachable with her there. She was already beginning to show the admirable character and qualities of a future Warrior. The two greeted each other cordially; it was polite, but with a cautious restraint. GD started the conversation by suggesting the meeting was unfairly coerced and never would have taken place otherwise. Even if there had been a long shot that she may be invited to discuss matters at his Manhattan office in the future, this was not the way to go about making that happen. Bella was the only reason for his being there. He went on to say that a child of Willow's age had nothing to talk about that would be of interest to him. He described himself as strictly a businessman who conducted his affairs responsibly and within the bounds of the law; his actions were beyond question or reproach.

Willow responded with a calm certainty, "Tell me why I should believe anything you say, since your actions have proven to be insensitive and self-serving in regard to the environment? The Disturbers have attempted to block our good intentions and efforts at cleaning up the planet at every turn. Young people will be the inheritors of the mess you leave. Now as its stewards, who are tasked with safeguarding this precious world, you're too blind and arrogant to see that it's dying. The highest good and greatest part of our mission is to stand ready in her defense, taking action when we see an environmental threat occurring. We've been very lucky so far when encountering your henchman on engagements. Yet, we know it would take a miracle to achieve a positive outcome if worse harm were to occur than has already been inflicted upon us."

Bella glowed and was smiling from ear to ear as she listened to Willow speak, since she knew her father had to listen under these circumstances. It was patently obvious to GD that his daughter's interest in the movement was more than simply a passing fancy. He considered that fact and chose his next words very carefully. "I appreciate what you've said here today, but forgive me, I'm a bit confused. What do you want from me? You have Arabella and, therefore, I'm respectfully obliged to listen to you."

A crack in his, otherwise, impenetrable façade, appeared opening the discussion up to more possibilities. Willow realized at that very moment she had a prime opportunity to get their message across, barter a truce, and hopefully work toward a better outcome between them. "We must, I believe, operate in the spirit of cooperation going forward. Take, for example, the pollution caused by your oil refinery in Texas. Emissions from the facility are at an all-time high. They contribute to poor air quality, which is unhealthy. If you would consider retrofitting with more efficient ventilation systems to decrease emissions, that kind of investment would be a move in the right direction toward a cleaner future for the planet."

"I get your point." He looked at Bella and replied, "We've been considering that option already. The Railroad Commission has been pressuring us to bring the plant up to code and to improve the standards of operation. That friend of yours, Rowdy, has been very effective in putting pressure on them. Actually, there is a tax incentive to do just that, which will net us a profit as well. It's a win-win situation for us. Now, are there any other concerns you would like to discuss?" GD sported a wry expression of greedy satisfaction, which resembled a cat when it's toying with a mouse its just caught.

"Well, there are only a couple more. Their names are Dumpster and Trasher. We've had many run-ins with them in places around the world while we were simply going about the important business of protecting the planet. On one specific occasion, our aquatic friend, Oceana, who's also a Warrior, narrowly missed being shot by a spear gun. That gun was fired by one of your henchmen. Our mission is a peaceful one, and even though we sometimes take great risks, we always practice non-violence in every engagement. I would ask respectfully that you not have them follow us and cause further problems."

GD was well aware that the two henchmen were employees of The Disturbers and at his behest. Bella looked sad as she stared at her father. "Is that true? Why are you trying to hurt them, Father?"

"My dear, it's much more complicated than you can possibly understand. I have business investments all around the world and they're being threatened from many directions. Those two protect my interests and provide me with an invaluable service."

"Yes, but Father, have you heard what Willow said about the mission of The Warriors? How can they be considered a threat if they're not harming anyone? Please, make it make sense, Father. I really want to know."

A noticeable sweat broke out on his forehead. "Bella, dear, they're at cross-purposes with our business ventures. Many times they interfere and get in the way when we're trying to move forward on a project. As I said before, it's complicated."

Willow thoughtfully interjected, "This is the time to address the worldwide climate crisis without delay. Our goal is to stand up to those who are actively doing harm to the planet. We go where we're needed and to the places that are under attack. Our philosophy has always been to work with businesses in a spirit of cooperation so that the destruction can end. We want to encourage communication and compromise to help the planet heal. We're open and receptive to rebuilding relations with your organization if you're willing."

"Well, for today anyway, I think we've talked enough." GD replied in a dismissive tone. "What's important is I've heard what you had to say and I'll give it my utmost attention and consideration." He looked down at his daughter and insisted firmly it was time to go. "Your adventure is over, my dear and now it's time to get you back home where it's safe." Bella quickly turned to Willow and whispered in her ear. "Will you say goodbye to the rest of The Warriors for me, especially Donald? Remember, I'll see you all again soon."

"Yes, Bella, I will. Please take care of yourself and know you have the heart of a Warrior." Bella hugged her tightly as GD looked on. It surprised him to witness the depth of emotion she showed to someone she barely knew and had only met a short while ago. The stretch limousine quickly departed and made haste toward the Queensboro Bridge and then onto Long Island. Willow stood by watching as they drove away thinking there had been a breakthrough on both sides. She feared, however, the conflict between them was far from over. It was a small victory and only time would tell how much progress was really made.

On the following day, The Warriors were set to have their meeting. Since they were spread out far and wide across the country and around the world, all the members weren't in attendance. Since it was convenient, they met at the office of billionaire, Sam Teyer, who was their financial support and benefactor. He was based primarily in California. However, he also had offices in lower Manhattan's financial district. He was always available to them on the spur of the moment.

Willow heartily greeted everyone at the meeting. She exclaimed with pride, "Wow...it's so good to see everybody today after the rally. It's really great to have everyone safe and sound and together again! Seeing each one of you is a real pleasure!"

Most of the collective was able to attend, but not all were there. Oceana and Zippy were back in Rhode Island with Bill taking it easy as winter was approaching. Of the members who were there, Willow felt inspired to be in the presence of such a diverse and talented group of individuals. Each one had committed their hands, hearts, and energies to the fullest extent and showed a deep devotion to the cause. It was a truly impressive sight to see. These were Willow's Warriors, she thought. That made her prouder than ever.

"We missed you too, Willow!" Gushed Sequoia. I'm so glad you're not in that lousy jail anymore!"

Juniper added, "Yeah, that was a close call! I guess Bella helped some too. Maybe, I misjudged her after all."

Willow replied in a reassuring tone, "Yep, maybe you did. When all is said and done, I think the two of you will become good friends. You're both made of the best material. Two strong and outspoken young women who have a lot to say."

The Anti-Fracks sat at the far end of the long table in the boardroom. While the guys leaned back, relaxing in their chairs, Rowdy sat forward, smiling from ear to ear. His eyes sparkled as he looked at Willow. The romantic feelings were emotionally charged and evident between them. The lovebirds tried to diffuse the explosive sparks, so as not to detract from the proceedings, but the passion they felt for one another wasn't easy to hide. It was crystal clear to the others. The Warriors observed the affection they had for one another. They appreciated how much stronger Willow and Rowdy were together and saw it as a positive sign. Inuk and Pan were in attendance, too. The Tempus Fugit arrived from the Arctic a couple of days before, safely delivering the two intrepid voyagers. As usual for this time of the year, a chill was in the air and delightfully colder temperatures were present. The fall weather in The Big Apple served as a pleasant reminder of home. It was the optimal climate for them to feel comfortable.

"Today, we'll be discussing the addition of new members to our ranks. I believe these candidates are worthy of our consideration. Let's meet them now, shall we?" Willow smiled as she introduced the visitors. "Everyone, I want to introduce you to Inuk and Pan. They're from Greenland. A while ago, I received a call from Richard Steffens, the American Glaciologist who has been in the Arctic measuring sea ice loss and the permafrost melt over the summer. He shared that he'd met twin brothers who are Inuit. He said they were interested in the environmental crisis and how it's been affecting their country. They've witnessed drastic changes on their island as a result of climate change and this persuaded them to become part of the movement. Their love of the natural world, as indigenous people, convinced me to invite them here so we could get to know them better. They've come from very far away to meet us." Willow gestured for them to stand. The boys looked shy as they stepped forward. They were uncomfortable in the company of strangers. Everyone welcomed the visitors with a warm applause.

Inuk was the first to speak. "Halu, unusakut." He said as he greeted the group with a friendly "good afternoon."

Rowdy rose to speak. "We've heard great things about you guys. Your culture seems super cool, especially hunting out in the wild and living off the land in harmony with nature. It sounds like a lot of fun!"

"Naturmiik." Panuk replied as he thanked him.

"Yeah, but it's a hard life too. We struggle to survive because our ways are disappearing. The people are losing the connection we once had with our island because of the melting ice. The young people have no purpose. There aren't any jobs and they can't get away from there as we've been fortunate enough to do. Many of our friends commit suicide because they feel hopeless."

A collective moan rose from the group. Willow looked concerned and quickly responded to the boys. "Your story is such a sad one, and even though we've all come from similar backgrounds, the difficult conditions and hopelessness you spoke of are hard to imagine. The Warriors are made up of unique individuals who are devoted to cleaning up the planet and standing up to Disturber forces. It's the highest purpose we can aspire to."

"We, too, love that idea! Panuk and I are committed to saving the planet along with the rest! We know what's going on is real because we see it happening in other environments around the world that are turning for the worse. We see the melting ice and the land underneath our home. This change is giving our people a way to work by farming and raising animals. However, we also know that the polar bears are dying too. This is not right." Inuk implored.

Pan added, "If we don't do something now, what little there is left will be gone. We can't stand by and watch everything we love die and do nothing about it."

The others remained silent as the two boys spoke. Each member had his or her own story to tell and what drove them to join the movement. The similarities and the desire to make a difference were the glue that bound them all together.

Willow concluded, "What we've heard from our new Inuit friends reminds us that we're all alike in some way. We have a common bond that holds us together, that is the love for our planet. We appreciate you both for sharing your thoughts and experiences with us today."

The boys thanked Willow and the rest for giving them the opportunity to come and find out more about The Warriors. There was a mutual sense in the room that their addition would be a welcome one.

Rowdy stood up again to speak. "I also wanted to bring another matter to everyone's attention. I have become aware of a group in Afghanistan called The Heat Seekers, who are actively resisting international oil interests in the northern part of the country. I believe they're facing Disturber forces in their homeland at great peril to themselves. I'm requesting permission to fly there and make contact."

"Do you think they would make a good addition to The Warriors, Rowdy?" Sequoia inquired.

"I don't know. I want to go there and locate them to find out."

Willow added, "Rowdy has made me aware of the group's activities and I think now would be a good time to go meet them. If they're willing to leave, bring them back to the US to see if they would be a good fit for The Warriors."

"Wow! I can't believe this is happening! First, Bella,

a couple of days ago and now today Inuk and Pan… I wonder who's next? The way I see it, we're going to be quite a force to be reckoned with! Look out, you Disturbers! This is so exciting! We're making history. I just know it!" Juniper shouted triumphantly.

Beaming as she looked around the room, Willow chuckled, "Yes, Juniper, this is a time of great expansion, growth and we're going to embrace it as a positive step going forward. It feels like we've chosen the most important work one can do. It will take all of our collective energies to achieve many of our plans. In that same spirit of growth and expansion, we must discuss some new ideas for the future and decide on those today too. Let's settle in and get down to business."

Chapter 13

War!

War! "I came, I saw, I conquered." - Julius Caesar

Afghanistan is a country long besieged by war. It was an ancient civilization that was hard to access geographically. Therefore, invaders found it difficult to control. It has never been conquered. In the modern era, many came and sought its valuable natural resources. Industrialized countries considered it a geologic motherlode and were greedy to plunder its untapped hidden treasures. This made for a persistent, tense and palpable antagonism toward intruders. After the Sept. 11th, 2001 terrorist attacks brought down the Twin Towers in New York City, the United States and NATO forces were seen as an unwelcome presence there. They punched a hole in the landscape and laid claim to the territory, imposing their military will in cities across the region. Occupation left the country exposed to exploitation on multiple levels.

The topography of the area was stark and inhospitable. It was a dry, barren desert landscape, with unremarkable features. As was the case in other exploited environments, the overall intrinsic value had yet to be explored. This made it of great importance to investors. Antiquities of time under pressure were cultivated and refined, bringing greedy opportunists from around the world. They wanted to exploit Afghanistan's untapped geologic wealth. Espoused by the West, under the questionable pretense of providing a democratic political system to the region, international oil conglomerates took advantage and seized upon a lucrative opportunity. The result was a groundswell of dissent among the civilian population, which played out significantly during the occupation as they looked to gain a monetary foothold in the Middle East.

The US and NATO exercised their considerable military might without sustaining much local opposition from the Taliban, who were the political and religious group in power. Those combined forces put a stranglehold on the country, placing it firmly under their power and control. It swung like a pendulum between local factions and those on the outside vying for dominance. There was ongoing chaos. A hostile atmosphere developed as a result. At the beginning of the incursion, air strikes and bombings were frequent and damaged the infrastructure of all major cities. The never-ending skirmishes that took place in and around Kabul polluted the air and groundwater. In addition, the physical and emotional health of the people deteriorated, manifesting in post-traumatic stress disorders, depression and anxiety. Consequently, the natural milieu and its citizens were under duress and in a constant state of unrest as they suffered through an incessant, heavy barrage. One reality remained a constant: the palpable and pervasive presence of war.

Homeless youth roamed free and unchecked in the streets, orphaned at an early age. These individuals learned about life the hard way. Functioning as a low-key type of resistance, they instituted their own homegrown brand of eco-terrorism against invading forces. The primary goal was to destroy or disable property as a form of protest, wanting to send a clear message to foreign concerns that they were not welcome. They poured on the pressure, disrupting the system in any way possible. It was an effective method to wield crude implements like metal pipes and rocks to break apart oil drilling machinery and vandalize rigs. However, these rouge gangs were frequently under the threat of danger if caught, but the risks involved were not a concern.

Mustafa and Abdullah were two such young men who engaged in this kind of activity. As teenagers, they grew up in an environment and country decimated by violence while unwittingly becoming vigilantes on a mission. They were deprived of family and friends due to landmines and bombings locally and across the region. Feeling disillusioned, with nothing left to lose, traumatized, in a perpetual state of fear and detached from grief, but willing to take matters into their own hands, they acted with bold impunity. Neither was from the same family. However, they shared a common experience. In 2010, when Abdullah was seven years old and Mustafa was eight years old, a bombing attack killed their parents making them orphans. This is when they first met. That year was considered the worst of the war as far as civilian casualties. Widespread indiscriminate hostilities occurred constantly. This was the norm and not the exception. Aid workers rescued and brought them to the Children's Village orphanage. The two soon bonded over their shared trauma. They became resilient, learning how to survive with limited resources in unstable conditions. Simultaneously, they cultivated a deep-seated hatred of an enemy whose presence in their country was perceived as intolerable. After becoming teenagers, they were eager to be independent of the orphanage, making a new home on the streets of Kabul. They were amateurs, but learned the art of sabotage, how to deface and destroy property, causing mischief and mayhem. They focused their attention on foreign interests, although their efforts were haphazardly applied. The military-industrial complex set up camp in the Jowzjan Province near the city of Sheberghan, which is north of Kabul; this was an area under exploration and considered one of the most promising oil-producing zones in the country. The area was beginning to become more densely populated with wells, so a plan was formulated that offered Mustafa and Abdullah an opportunity to join a band of dissenters known as The Heat Seekers. They were actively engaged in disrupting the operations of fuel providers in the area. That summer, the two young men utilized a secret, underground network for transitioning by making their way to the north.

They hitched a ride for the ten-hour drive to Sheberghan with a Red Cross truck that was delivering food and other supplies. This allowed them to travel for free and go, for the most part, unnoticed. It was the safest way to get to their final destination with the least amount of difficulty. The plan was to rendezvous with a man named Omar. He was about twenty years old and the leader of the cabal. Mustafa and Abdullah arrived in the middle of summer. It was not uncommon for temperatures to reach into the mid 100's, making conditions uncomfortable. The truck made its last stop at a makeshift refugee camp to deliver relief supplies in Sheberghan. They thanked the driver for the ride and departed hastily in the direction of the city in order to locate Omar. By making careful inquiries of common street merchants who pointed them in the general direction, they proceeded to a local park.

Bokhdi Amusement Park was one such place where interested parties could visit and find someone. At the park, locals went to relax and ride bumper cars, the Merry-Go-Round and enjoy other attractions. Mustafa and Abdullah made their way straight to the center of the park. This was where men could congregate, talk politics and socialize with each other. Youth, like themselves, were also seen hanging around looking for fun playing arcade games along the midway. Ever alert and watchful, they stood conspicuously in the open, keeping their eyes peeled to make contact with Omar.

He was described as a man of a slight build who had a modest beard befitting his age. After waiting only a short while, an individual matching that description casually approached, speaking Pashto, the official language.

He asked, "Are you looking for someone?"

"Yes, we are. Is your name Omar?"

Without supplying an answer, he replied, "Let's take a walk. Are you hungry?" The two nodded vigorously as if they hadn't eaten in days. They followed the man to an open-air market where food vendors sold their wares. They chose to have a bowl of korma and kabuli palaw which was a tasty stew with rice. Both were famished after such a long ride and appreciated the meal.

As Mustafa and Abdullah inhaled their food, Omar inquired. "How was your trip? You arrived here after quite a long journey. That's a great accomplishment."

Mustafa began, "It was alright, but uncomfortable. The Red Cross made a lot of delivery stops along the way, but we were able to get up, go out, and stretch our legs once in a while."

Licking his lips while finishing the stew, Abdullah added, "They were ok…friendly for foreigners."

"We welcome your help in the struggle against these invaders. They're a curse in our country!! Our work is to drive them out forever!" Mustafa and Abdullah spontaneously cried out, "Allahu Akbar!" It's a common chant of solidarity in Middle Eastern countries, which helped to convince Omar they were committed to his cause.

In the following weeks, they studied the techniques that other members used in engagements that were focused solely on sabotaging oil extraction efforts in the Jowzjan Province. The activities of The Heat Seekers came to the attention of the local Afghan National Police. The Disturber Forces made up of US and European business interests, sanctioned the police to act on their behalf. Those interests included the Frick and Frack Oil Corporation, part of an international conglomerate that was vying for control of mineral rights in the desert.

The existence of Disturber forces in the Middle East, in this case, Afghanistan, came to Rowdy's attention, partly because he was keeping a close watch on the activities of the F&F Corporation. The Anti-Fractivists monitored their movements around the world as they related to oil. They became highly concerned when those who were deemed a threat, due to their history of ecological exploitation, showed an interest in a specific area. The Warriors operated in the spirit of non-violence and practiced a tamer version of eco-terrorism. They applied pressure to the status quo on issues through their presence. Their philosophy of peaceful activism centered around protest as a form of resistance. Their approach involved applying pressure to big business and the political system as a preferred means to bring about change. The Heat Seekers, by comparison, lived in a constant state of war. They were bombarded by hostile forces as their country's geologic wealth was ripe for picking and up for grabs. In these desperate times, drastic measures were required because conflict begat extraordinary action.

Willow stood by nervously, waiting for the flight to Mazar I Sharif International Airport to board at JFK. "Do you have everything you need, Rowdy? Is your ticket in order? I asked Sam to have a private jet ready for the flight over, but he told me he could only arrange one on short notice for the flight home." Looking worried, she added, "I wish you didn't have to fly today. Maybe the weather won't be so good. It might not be safe, you know? You'll be traveling for almost a day just to get there, dammit! Please tell me again why you have to travel halfway around the world?"

Rowdy slid his arm around her shoulder and clutched it tightly to provide some comfort and reassurance. "I'm going there to find The Heat Seekers, who are resistance fighters standing up to the oil industry in Afghanistan. They might want to join our ranks and become part of The Warriors. I have to connect with them to find out. Now, do you remember what I said to you in jail, babe? I need you in my life. You're stuck with me. So, stop worrying. This is just another engagement and I've been on them before." He grinned while attempting to de-escalate the tension in his usual playful way.

Fretting while holding back the tears, she struggled with her emotions. "Rowdy, this is different; Afghanistan is a war zone…IT'S NOT SAFE!"

"My love, we're Warriors. You taught me that. We travel the world, taking a stand for the environment, taking on Disturber forces wherever and whenever we're needed. It's nothing new, right, babe? Just another assignment."

Shuddering at the thoughts that were racing through her head, Willow feared the worst, that she would never see him again. Looking deeply into his soulful, sea-green eyes, she confided, "I know I'm young and inexperienced in the ways of the world, as I've been told so often by Mother, but you remind me of home which is the only safe place I know and where I belong. Don't ever leave me, Rowdy! Never! This journey would be empty, as I would be, without you!" Unable to gain her composure, she began to cry.

He hugged her tightly, returning her feelings while putting on a brave face. "We have a bond that can't be broken, babe. The day I met you was the luckiest day of my life. We're both young and inexperienced. There is nothing wrong with that. Now, don't worry, sweetheart, I'll be fine. I'll call you as soon as I arrive." As the boarding call came over the loudspeaker, Willow clung to him tightly afraid to let go. They embraced while walking slowly toward the gate. "I'll be fine, babe. Will you trust me that I can handle myself out there?"

"Yes, whatever you say, my darlin'. I trust you. You will call me as soon as you land, though, won't you?"

Rowdy laughed. "Of course! Oh, I completely forgot there's something I want to ask you before I take off. Will you marry me?"

Momentarily at a lost for words, she shrieked. "Wait a minute! What?"

"You heard me, you always do." Pausing for effect, he added, "Well, Ms. O'Brien, yes or no? Will you be my wife?" He stared at her intently, searching for an answer, while passengers strolled past, observing their tender scene. Preparing to board the plane, he implored impatiently, “Look, they're not going to hold the flight forever… what will it be?”

Could this really be happening? She was unable to speak, momentarily stunned, as she stuttered, “I, I love you, Rowdy!”

He happily shouted as he boarded the plane, “Just think about it. You don’t have to decide now. I’ll call you when I get there, babe! I love you, too!”

The flight to Mazur I Sharif proved to be a tediously long affair. As predicted, it took approximately sixteen hours with a short layover in Istanbul en route to Afghanistan. When Rowdy was finally on the ground and going through customs, he claimed tourism as the reason for his visit. He arranged a taxi to take him the rest of the way, as he made a quick call to Willow to let her know he was alright and to put her mind at ease. It was another two hours by car to Sheberghan, where he was hoping to locate The Heat Seekers. Rowdy was relieved to discover that the driver spoke English quite well and they were able to communicate. It was important to find out more about what was going on in the country at present so he could successfully complete the mission.

The driver’s name was Mohammed. He was rough-hewn and weather-beaten, but had a genuinely pleasant, friendly nature. “Since the foreigners come to our country, it has been very difficult. They try to change the way we live, as well as our culture, politics, how we dress and what we think. They want to rule us and tell us what to do," Mohammed observed.

"Is that so bad? What was it like under the Taliban?" Rowdy inquired.

"They were also hard on the people and determined to have control, but they're Afghan people, like me. We share the same culture. But, what do I know? I'm a simple man. I drive my taxi here or there. I don't ask questions… They pay me so I can make a living and take care of my family. That's all I know."

"Since I don't speak the language, Mohammed, will you serve as my guide and interpreter? I'll pay you well for your services."

"It depends, Rowdy. By the way, what kind of a name is Rowdy? I've never heard one like that before."

"Do you know about the great state of Texas in the U.S.A? That's where I'm from. It's a common name down there." He replied proudly.

"Oh, yes! You must be a cowboy, right?"

"Not exactly. I'm an environmental activist on a mission to save the planet. That's what brings me to Afghanistan. I'm looking for a group known as The Heat Seekers. Have you heard of them?"

Mohammed pulled the car over and came to an abrupt halt. "Do you know what you ask of me? They're wanted by the Afghan National Police as terrorists. I don't desire any trouble."

Thinking carefully before he spoke, Rowdy responded, "Once we get to Sheberghan, you can take me to where I can make some inquiries. Your service, my friend, ends there. I shall not put you in any further danger."

"Rowdy, you're a young man and a foreigner with red hair and spots all over your face! You don't even have a beard!" Rowdy sported a 5 o'clock shadow, but since he was so fair-skinned, it was faint and barely visible. "I know of an amusement park in the city where men get together to meet and talk. It should be alright for us to go there. Don't worry. I'll help you, my friend." Offered Mohammed, "But we must be very careful."

"Those 'spots' are called freckles. I inherited them from my father". Offering his appreciation, he said, "Thank you for your help. I know you're risking a lot getting involved with someone you just met and don't know."

Mohammed smiled while nodding in agreement. "Okay, cowboy, we understand each other now. Let's be on our way before dark."

Chapter 14

The Long Way Home

"You cannot reason with a tiger when your head is in its mouth." - Winston Churchill

Upon arriving in Sheberghan, the taxi proceeded to the Bokhdi Amusement Park. The two made their way through the park to its center and the common meeting grounds. Rowdy was wearing a black hoodie to hide his copper locks in an attempt to blend into the surroundings. It was a bit of wishful thinking on his part, hoping the subterfuge would work; otherwise, it could be extremely dangerous.

Mohammed approached a group of men and spoke in Pashto. He greeted them with, "Salaam, wradz mo pa kheyr." This meant hello and good afternoon. Rowdy remained uncharacteristically silent, playing it cool. He kept his head down and stood nearby. He purposely didn't get too close and waited patiently in the shadows.

Mohammed made his inquiries discreetly and quickly. He conducted Rowdy out of the park and back to the safety of the taxi as fast as he could.

"What did they tell you, Mohammed?"

"They told me very little. They told me only the name of a man and to ask for him in the marketplace. The man's name is Omar."

Rowdy implored, "Let's go! I think we're on the right track!"

"Now, wait a minute! You must remember where you are. Don't ever forget that. We'll go, but slowly and always to be safe. Okay, my friend?"

Sporting a satisfied grin, he replied, "I'll follow, you lead, Mohammed." Rowdy was headstrong and a bit reckless and was an experienced protester, but this was different. He was smart enough to know better than to charge into a conflict zone, which may result in dire consequences for himself and his companion. Gratefully, he took Mohammed's advice.

They located the marketplace in the center of the city. It was set up more like a bazaar, a little rough around the edges. Street merchants of all kinds crowded each corner and sold everything from fruits and vegetables, meat and cheeses, to clothing, such as tunics and other garments. They also sold brightly colored kites of all shapes and sizes. The art of kite making and flying was highly prized in the country. It was a simple pleasure that had become the number one recreational activity. A feast for the senses of sight and sound.

The two men strolled casually and wandered

through the busy street, as Mohammed occasionally stopped to converse with a vendor. They were extremely cautious when inquiring regarding the whereabouts of The Heat Seekers or Omar, hoping to get a lead as they proceeded on their way. Since Rowdy hadn't eaten for hours, they stopped at a stand that served falafels and other Middle Eastern fare. Each had a sample platter of food and a strong cup of coffee. As they stood eating, an elderly man wearing a kaftan and turban approached.

Speaking in Pashto, he greeted them, "Salaam, my name is Amir. Are you the ones looking for Omar? If yes, would you follow me? I'll take you to meet him."

They followed closely, making their way down a dusty, narrow side street into a dead-end alley that led to a plain-looking door. The man knocked and then turned around, saying, "Da khoday pa amaan." He bade them a hasty goodbye and quickly scurried away.

Mohammed cautioned Rowdy to stifle his urge to speak and to let him do all the talking. The door opened and a thin young man with a sparse beard appeared. "Salaam, my name is Omar. I hear you've been asking around about me. What can I do for you?"

"Salaam, we were looking for The Heat Seekers and were told you knew how to find them."

Omar nodded in the affirmative and bade them to come inside. The two walked into a room of young men who were sitting, squatting and standing. They appeared to be about Rowdy's age and not more than twenty years old or so. All wore a stern look of determination, hardened by life, which was odd considering they were so young.

Omar introduced the group as The Heat Seekers. "Now, why have you come here looking for us?" He had no difficulty speaking English.

This time Rowdy responded, removing his hoodie, exposing his orangish red shoulder-length hair. "I'm an environmental activist from America and part of a group known as The Warriors. We're young people, like yourselves, dedicated to take a stand against Disturber forces exploiting the Earth for profit. In your country, as in ours, the oil industry is busy drilling with no regard for the land other than how it can be used. We've been all around the world and this is true everywhere we go."

Omar focused his attention on Mohammed. "And why are you here?"

"I drive a taxi. That's all. I'm lending a hand to my young friend."

Rowdy continued, "The Warriors are aware of your activities and want to help you in any way we can. Both of us are working towards the same end, which is the protection and survival of the planet."

"Yes, but we're fighting the foreigners who have invaded our country and you're one of them! Allahu Akbar!" The rest of the men stood up, echoing his cry.

Rowdy was impressed with the display of fervent loyalty. Praising their dedication to the cause, he said, "I admire that. We're committed and believe as you do also."

Omar yelled, "What do you know, American? Are

you aware of our struggles? Many in our group are orphans and have lost their families at the hands of the military from your country." He pointed at Abdullah and Mustafa and shouted, "Like these two!"

Mohammed became nervous as he watched Omar getting more agitated while speaking. He quietly gestured for them to leave.

Rowdy waved him off, "I got this."

He turned back to Omar and appealed, "I understand your hatred for those who come here uninvited and steal what's not rightfully theirs. I see it all over the world. They're Disturber forces who only care about money and nothing else. It's the reason we formed The Warriors, to stand up against tyranny over people, animals and the land. We're working with you in the struggle. Many brothers and sisters all over the world know what's happening here and want to lend their support."

Mustafa and Abdullah listened closely as Rowdy spoke. Whispering to his friend, Abdullah asked, "What do you think of the red-headed one?"

"He's strange. What he says makes me wonder. Do you think there are others who fight in their country as we do here to rid themselves of foreigners?"

Before Abdullah could answer, Omar bellowed, "You speak of wanting to help us. Do you mean what you say?"

Rowdy replied confidently, "Yes, I do. How can I prove that to you?"

"We will go to the oilfield tonight. If you mean what you say, you can go with us."

"Alright, I accept."

Mohammed grabbed Rowdy's arm and pulled him aside, "Hold on, my friend! Do you know what you're doing? These are wanted men!"

"I came here to find them, Mohammed, and with your help, I have. I want you to leave me here, okay? Go back to Masur I Sharif. I'll call you in a day or two to come pick me up."

"Rowdy, are you sure? It's not safe and it could get very dangerous." Mohammed implored.

"You sound just like my wife back home." Rowdy shared, "She said the same thing to me right before I left."

"You're so young to have a wife, my friend. She's right. What's her name?"

"Willow. I asked her to marry me just before I came here, but she didn't give me an answer." Rowdy confessed.

"I think you should leave this place. Go back home, where it's safe and get married."

"Soon. I'll call you, Mohammed, to pick me up in a day, alright?"

"No, Rowdy. I'll stay in Sheberghan for that extra day. I need to take a break anyway, and who knows, you may need me sooner than you think." They shook hands as they spoke.

Mohammed gave Rowdy his number and wished him good luck before he departed.

He stood in the midst of a group of young men who he

couldn't relate to or understand and wondered if they were a militant band or just inspired youth as committed to protecting their country as he was about his home state of Texas. It was at this very moment he thought of Willow. She never did answer his question. Why did she hesitate? Was she in love with him as much as he was with her? What if he didn't make it back home and never saw her again? He was in a temporary daze. The racing thoughts flooded his mind, and the stress of the situation brought them on. Giving himself a pep talk, he snapped back and refocused his attention on the reason for being there.

Omar berated Rowdy, cackling loudly, "I see you, American. You're not sure this is safe! What have you gotten yourself into, right? Well, it isn't! Go home and get out of my country!"

He confirmed, "No, I'm here as a friend, Omar. As I said before, I understand you and know your struggle is real."

"We'll see tonight whether your words mean anything or not. For now, rest. We will leave when it's dark."

He attempted to close his eyes and get some sleep as his host had suggested, but Rowdy felt a tug on his sleeve. It was Mustafa and Abdullah. They were sitting up, staring hard at him. They looked as though they were burning with questions.

Rowdy smiled, "Hi. Do you speak English?"

"Yes, I speak some." He pointed at his friend, "This is Abdullah and I'm Mustafa. We're Heat Seekers."

"Why are you called that? Does it have something to do with living in the desert?"

Abdullah answered, "Omar says we're nomads wandering in the hot desert seeking truth." Mustafa nodded in agreement.

Rowdy inquired, "How long have you been with The Heat Seekers?"

"Not long, only two months." Mustafa inched his body closer to Rowdy's, "Can you tell us more about The Warriors?"

"What do you want to know?"

Abdullah asked, "Who's in your group?"

Rowdy replied, "The Warriors are made up of young men, like yourselves and young women, too."

"No! How can you allow women in your group? Females don't belong there!" Mustafa declared, "Do they wear their burkas?"

"The Warriors accept everyone, whether man or woman, as human beings who will inherit the Earth. All of us have a stake in the future survival of the planet. It's important for each one to participate equally."

Rowdy explained their purpose with a compassionate understanding so as to honor the differences between the cultures. He realized it wouldn't be a good idea to disclose right now that their leader was a woman. He thought this could be done at another time and place, perhaps. It would better serve the cause then.

Omar approached the three as they spoke, "The time has come for us to go, as it will be dark soon. Get yourselves ready."

A company of eight men, including Rowdy, assembled in preparation for the night's escapade. Under cover of darkness, they departed. They were careful not to be seen, as most were wanted for various acts of vandalism by the Afghan National Police. Their destination was the Zomrad Sai oilfield, which was just slightly over an hour from Sheberghan. They traveled in two separate cars, which were a short distance apart so as not to draw attention to themselves. Rowdy rode in a foursome that included Abdullah, Mustafa and Omar. They spoke Pashto amongst themselves. From their body language, it appeared that Omar was giving detailed instructions about what to do once they arrived. What Rowdy gathered, observing Omar's gestures, was that they had only been part of The Heat Seekers for a couple of months, and therefore, still in training. Both were still novices and not officially in the group yet. Everything they were planning to do was against The Warriors non-violent stance. As Rowdy was riding along in the car on Ring Road, he prayed for a miracle that would spare him from dishonoring that pledge.

They drove, finally coming to the outskirts of the city enroute to their destination. This journey was considered potentially hazardous at night due to the unpredictability of the road's safety. Marauder ambushes, law enforcement and military forces added to the difficulty of the trip. It was clear to Rowdy that anything could potentially happen under these circumstances. The first car was approximately thirty seconds ahead in order to keep at a safe distance. As they rounded a corner, a flash of red and white lights exposed a stopped car. It was the other vehicle that had been pulled over. The Afghan National Police had been waiting. Most likely, an informant had tipped them off for money, providing the inside track on where they could be found. Rowdy, relieved, had received his miracle, although far from out of danger. Omar shut the lights off. Slowly, backing up, he turned the car around headed in the direction of the house.

"I think this has something to do with you, American! You must have been seen and reported. You brought them to us! The others have been caught now and could go to prison! What do you say about that!"

Rowdy sat quietly. He chose his words carefully before speaking. "I realize that my presence may have attracted attention, but I think your methods, responding with violence, made you wanted by the authorities. Every time you go against a superior force in an aggressive manner, you risk being arrested. If it's not today, then another time. My presence only brought it about sooner, that's all." Omar scowled at Rowdy as he drove on. The rest of the ride was punctuated by a deadly silence.

Driving at a fast pace through the city streets, they soon arrived at the house. The four men went quickly inside. Omar turned to Mustafa and Abdullah with instructions in Pashto, "Watch him until I get back. I'll return in an hour! I must go to check on the others." He glared at Rowdy as he looked straight at him, "I'll deal with you later!"

The three sat without speaking for a short while. Finally, Mustafa spoke up. "We like you, Rowdy. This is not easy for us."

"It's unpleasant for me too. Can you tell me what is going to happen?"

Abdullah hesitated before speaking. He and Mustafa talked among themselves. Rowdy inferred from their body language that they couldn't decide whether or not to answer his question.

"We're afraid to say anything, because Omar may get angry. He would not like us to help you, except we don't want to see you get hurt."

"Why? What did he mean when he said, *I'll deal with you later?*"

Abdullah clarified, "Omar knows people who hate foreigners. He will turn you over to them."

Rowdy thanked them for their honesty. "I'm sorry I made things difficult for you, but I'm glad you decided to tell me. I need to get back home safely because there are people waiting for my return who care about me. Do you understand?"

Mustafa replied, "I lost my family when I was young, so did Abdullah. We're orphans."

"You have no one who cares about you?" Rowdy asked.

"No, all we have is each other. I'm seventeen and Abdullah is sixteen."

"You guys would make a great addition to The Warriors. As far as I'm concerned, growing up in a war zone makes you a good candidate. I want to invite both of you to join us. But we have to hurry now. I have a cab standing by to take us back to Masur I Sharif. There we can catch a plane to the US. Are you coming with me?"

Neither could believe what they were hearing. "Do you mean it, Rowdy? You don't know anything about us."

Rowdy nervously paced the floor, hoping not to run into Omar again. He cautioned, "Let's just say I'm a good judge of character. You guys don't belong here, breaking the law and getting in trouble. There are much better ways of taking a stand for the environment. I'll teach you. If we're going, we've got to go now, though, ok?"

An odd, quizzical expression appeared on Mustafa's face. He nodded his head yes as he spoke in a clear voice, "It's strange that you ask, but if you want us, we will go with you, Rowdy."

"Great choice! Now, let's get the hell out of here!" He exclaimed as he motioned for them to grab their stuff to make a quick departure.

Rowdy punched in the number Mohammed had given him, hoping he'd still pick up his phone and be in the city.

He answered very relieved to hear from him, "Rowdy, I've been waiting, my friend. I'm so glad you called."

"Can you meet us at Bokhdi Amusement Park in 15 minutes?"

"Us?"

"Yes, us. I'll explain everything on the drive to the

airport."

"I'll be there, leaving now!"

The three beat a hasty retreat away from the house. They carefully traversed along the city streets, making good time getting to the park without encountering any difficulties. The taxi was waiting by the entrance. Mohammed got out and helped Mustafa and Abdullah into the back seat while Rowdy rode up front.

"Thank you for coming to the rescue again, my friend."

"It's my pleasure and all part of the service." Mohammed said with a smile. "Now, let's get moving!"

The car pitched up and down as it sped away toward Asian Highway 76 from Sheberghan to Masur I Sharif. It was a familiar route and one that Mohammed knew well.

"Tell me, Rowdy, why have you brought these two with you? You know they won't be able to leave the country."

"We'll be flying home on a private jet that is standing by ready at the airport."

"Yes, but they will have to get through customs to leave the country." Mohammed pointed out.

Rowdy reached for his cell phone and replied, "I'm going to make a call to see if I can straighten that out right now."

The phone rang a few times before Willow answered, "Hi, my sweet love. Sorry, I wasn't able to reach out to you sooner. I've had my hands full here."

"Oh, Rowdy! I missed you so much! I'm so happy to hear your voice!" Willow gushed.

"Yes, I missed you too, babe. We're heading to Masur I Sharif now. I need your help. Can you contact Sam and make sure we clear customs and have the plane waiting for us at the airport?"

"It sounds like you connected with The Heat Seekers?"

"I did, babe. Their names are Abdullah and Mustafa. I want you to meet them soon, but we gotta get home first!"

"I'm so proud of you and thankful you're safe! I'll call Sam and arrange everything right now. Have a good flight, my love. We've got a lot to talk about when you get home." Before Rowdy could respond, she'd already hung up.

As she said she would, Willow removed any obstacles for getting back into the US. Before he left Masur I Sharif for the flight home, Rowdy thanked Mohammed for all his help and support on the journey. Mohammed let him know that the next time he was in Afghanistan visiting, he should look him up.

The flight was long and uneventful. It was a far cry from where they'd been and a great relief to be safe. The two young men were fascinated by every part of the plane and the fact that they were in the sky at all, flying, was oddly amazing to them. They'd never experienced anything like this before.

Willow stood by solemnly. Her nose pressed tightly against the window. It seemed like a lifetime. Sequoia, Juniper, Donald and Julian were there to welcome him home too. The flight arrived that next morning at JFK.

The Warriors watched eagerly as Rowdy came through the gate with the newcomers.

Willow caught sight of him and couldn't contain herself. She started running towards him, holding back tears of joy and shouting "Rowdy!"

"Don't worry, babe. I'm here. Did you think I wouldn't make it?" He asked while lovingly caressing her.

"I'm so glad you're home! We all missed you so much!"

Donald and Julian enthusiastically shook his hand as Sequoia and Juniper gave him hugs. Rowdy introduced Mustafa and Abdullah to the group. They prayerfully bowed politely and greeted the others with "Salaam." Juniper stuck her hand out for them to shake. However, both were too stunned at the sight of such a bold female to respond. Rowdy watched the encounter with great amusement.

"These men are known as The Heat Seekers. I hope we can welcome them into our ranks so they can become Warriors like us. We will get to know them better later on today. Now, all I want to do is get out of here and go home!"

As they walked arm and arm, Willow's resting her head on Rowdy's shoulder, he whispered, "Well, have you thought about my question? Will you be my wife?"

With a wry smile on her face, she replied, "Oh, I don't know…I thought we could live together instead."

"Don't tease me! You're kidding, right?"

"What's wrong with living together? Lots of people

do it." Willow burst out laughing, quickly dissolving into tears.

"There's no other man for me. I have blinders on and can see only you. It has been that way from the moment we met. Your warm smile and generous heart. You're so giving and compassionate. You're the dearest soul and always there to protect us, while standing up for what's right and good. I'm blessed, I know it. Whatever direction I go in, or path I follow, I want you by my side, forever. Yes, I'll be your wife, a thousand times yes!"

Rowdy hesitated for a moment before flashing his famous smile. Chuckling to himself, he replied, "A simple yes would have sufficed."

They laughed and then kissed while holding each other closely in a tender embrace before running to catch up with the others.

Mother sat back, watching. Feeling satisfied and comfortable observing from afar the unfolding of a miracle. The planet's renewal and protection were in good hands. Though the existential crisis appeared far from over and Disturber forces were still lurking, she knew this momentum shift could only be interpreted as a positive sign. It was due to the efforts of young people from around the world who were striving onward to make a difference in the dust and waste of humanity. This was a sign of great hope, for it was combined with a staunch determination to never let this happen again. Mother knew there would be much more to look forward to. There were many paths yet to tread, but at this moment, the pride would be enough to carry through.

Willow's Warriors Trilogy

The adventures of Willow's Warriors pursuing and fighting for a better world will continue in the sequel, The Enablers.